And Then Love

Willow Hall Romance, Book 1
A Pride and Prejudice Variation Prequel
The events in this novella happen prior to the beginning of *Pride and Prejudice*.

~*~*~

She needs a rescue. He's her only hope.

Chapter 1

The sun's rays were sliding toward the horizon as Lucy Tolson folded the letter. A slight breeze dashed by and tried to snatch the paper from her. Lucy tucked it into her pocket. How long she had sat there, reading and considering that letter, she did not know. It had come earlier in the day, but she had refused to open it until she would be able to share it with her father for she knew the news it contained would not be welcome.

"It is as you said, Papa. Uncle will take me in two months' time if I have not found a suitable husband before then." Lucy leaned her head against the coolness of her father's headstone and spoke to the fresh mound of earth that covered him where he lay beside her mother. Two months? She shook her head. She would be lucky if her uncle did not come for her within the week. Not that he cared for her! No, his interest in her, as it was in everything in his life, had always been mercenary. He had proven that long ago.

"I'll not be separated from you, Papa." She laid a hand

on the earthen mound. "I could not abide living in his house with that woman and those children. And my money, Papa, you know he would not care for it as you have. It would be gone within a card game along with my chances for a good match." She pulled her handkerchief from her pocket to catch her tears. "I cannot go with him, Papa. You know what he is." She buried her face in the bit of cloth she held and let her grief and fears flow freely for a few moments. Then, after several shuddering breaths, she lifted her face to her father's marker once again. "I will consider all you have told me. I will make a good choice, and even if I am not loved as Mama was, I will be happy."

"Miss Tolson?" From a window in the church, Philip Dobney had seen the lady enter the graveyard and was worried because she had stayed for so long. For the past few minutes, he had been watching her weep from the window as the sermon he had been practising sat neglected on a pew a few feet away. He knew that grief was a demanding master, who ran roughshod over many, sometimes, leading them to consider all sorts of things they would not have considered when in a happier state. And it was always strongest at first, so he knew that Lucy's grief was great. It had been but a few days since Mr. Tolson had been buried. It was the first service of that sort which he had performed since accepting the living here in Kympton.

Lucy accepted his hand and with his help rose from

where she knelt. "I am well, Mr. Dobney. I was just sharing some news with Papa." She dried her eyes and allowed him to guide her to the bench next to the church.

"Please call me Philip," he said, taking a seat next to her. "We have known each other for years, and at times such as these, I believe we can be less formal. Can we not be?" Indeed, Lucy and his sister Mary Ellen had been friends since before they were in leading strings.

His mother and Mrs. Tolson were often in each other's gardens or sitting rooms when he was young. They would have tea and stitch while their daughters would play. More than once, he had been enlisted to help keep them from trouble so that their mothers could relax.

They had been tolerably good and pleasant enough to have as companions for a while. He and his friends had actually come to like having them around on occasion.

"Very well, but on Sundays and in company, I shall insist on calling you Mr. Dobney." She smiled at him as she sniffled and stuffed her handkerchief into her pocket. "And you, of course, may call me Lucy." She drew a deep breath and released it. Her heart felt less heavy and oddly protected as she sat there with him. But then, that was how his presence had always made her feel.

"You have settled into the position of parson well." She gave him a sidelong look. "My father commented on how he has enjoyed your sermons these last few weeks. I believe he called them refreshing."

"Lucy, I am here to offer comfort to you, not garner your praise." He chuckled.

"Passing on my father's praise gives me comfort. It makes it seem less like he is gone."

"Then, I shall attempt to receive his compliments graciously." He leaned back and looked toward the grave next to which she had been kneeling. "You said you were sharing news with your father. Is it anything with which I could be of assistance?"

She tilted her head and gave him a searching look. She had promised her father that she would speak to each of the men on his list. However, she had intended to do so with her Aunt Tess present, not while alone in a churchyard.

"Anything at all, Lucy," he prompted.

Her cheeks grew warm, and she pulled up her shoulders and let them fall in a little shrug. "There is nothing." She paused, then allowed the rest of her thought to rush out before she could think better of it. "Unless you wish to marry me or know of someone else who would be willing."

Before he could respond to her comment, she pulled a folded paper from her pocket. "There is a list." She thrust it at him, keeping her eyes focused on the paper that wavered in her shaking hand. She did not wish to see whatever expression he might be wearing.

"I made it with Papa just last week," she explained. "I

listed all the gentlemen who were of marriageable age and according to my sources, looking to take a wife."

Philip rolled his eyes as he began to unfold the paper. By sources, she, no doubt, meant his sister. Mary Ellen always seemed to know everything that was going on in their village. She was not a gossip, but she was a listener with a keen memory, sharing what she had heard only when she felt it would benefit him in dealing with some person or situation.

"You will note," said Lucy quickly as she watched his fingers smooth out the creases, "that most of the names have been crossed off. In fact, Papa left only two choices whom he deemed acceptable, but since Mr. Pryce seems well on his way to speaking to Miss Burton's father, I removed his name. It can be added again should he be unsuccessful with Mr. Burton, although that is highly unlikely." She bit her lip and swallowed nervously as he opened the final fold.

Philip scanned the list of names that had been scratched out. There were little notes next to each with a reason for their removal. As he reached the bottom of the list, his eyes grew wide as they read the one remaining name — Philip Dobney.

"There is a second list on the right." Lucy's finger trembled slightly as she pointed to it. "Reasons I would make an excellent parson's wife."

He looked at her and shook his head trying to grasp what was happening.

"Please, just read it," she whispered.

So, he did.

She had been thorough and accurate. There was not a thing on that list which was not true. She was practical. She was capable of finding solutions to problems — even ones others had deemed unsolvable. She was seldom given to fits of nerves or swooning. Things that had shocked his sister, had failed to rouse more than a laugh, a scold, or a suggestion for improvement of a prank from her. But, he glanced at her, she had always been full of advice when asked. He smiled as he returned his attention to the list and saw that she had included that as the second to last point.

His breath caught in his chest and unexpected tears sprang to his eyes as he read the last point.

My father had confidence in me.

It was a statement that though short in length was filled with volumes of commentary on her character. Philip knew that Lucy's father had relied on her heavily since her mother died three years ago, and Simon Tolson was an upstanding man who was revered by many, including Philip. If Mr. Tolson had confidence in someone, there was a good reason. Though the man was gracious and kind, his approval was hard earned.

Philip scanned the list one more time as he thought.

He could not refute any of the points, least of all the last one. He began to refold the list. If both Mr. Tolson and his daughter, who was much like her father, thought she would make him a good wife, then there was no doubt in his mind that she was well-prepared and would do him credit. It would do him well to, at least, consider it.

"You have heard of my uncle?" Lucy asked quietly.

Philip nodded. Lucy's uncle was the only person he had ever heard his mentor, Mr. Harker, speak about harshly, and for good reason. Angus Tolson was the exact opposite of his brother — Cain and Able, Mr. Harker called them. Where Simon sought to do what was right, Angus sought a way around it.

"I shall be required to go live with him at the end of two months' time unless I have a husband. I cannot abide him and have no wish to live with him or his wife, nor do I have a desire to take care of his children — I have met them, and they are quite unpleasant."

Her voice grew stronger as she spoke of her uncle, and Philip watched her posture stiffen and her countenance grow agitated.

She turned toward him. "And my money, which is supposed to go to my future husband, will, without a doubt, be gambled away. It is what he does with any bit of money he receives."

Desperation filled her eyes, and Philip could hear the fear that crept into her voice.

"I will then become useless to him — a burden." Lucy tried to force away the panic that filled her. "I will be given to whichever gentleman is willing to pay the highest price to have me as a wife." She shook her head slowly. "You are my only hope for a good match, but I would rather marry Mr. Gibson or Mr. Scott and turn a blind eye to a mistress than go to live with my uncle."

His head bobbed up and down as he considered her words. From the stories Mr. Harker had told him, her life with her uncle would be as bleak as she described. It was not something he wished for her. The guilt of knowing he could have saved her from such a fate but chose not to was not something he wished to endure, and he was certain that his sister would make sure he felt his guilt keenly.

He finished folding the paper and then looked into her desperate eyes. How could he refuse her when to see her so fearful caused his chest to constrict and his heart to hurt? She needed a husband, and he did need a wife. Mr. Harker had been impressing that on him for some time. He saw no reason why it should not be Lucy. She had proven her qualifications, and although she was not considered by many to be a beauty, her features and figure were pleasing and womanly.

"There is one thing missing from your list." He handed it back to her. Her brows drew together in confusion. "I should like to know if you think we could enjoy the intimacy of marriage."

Her eyebrows shot up in surprise, and her mouth popped open.

"I would not have expected you to know or to have actually written such a thing on your list, of course." He felt his ears growing warm. "But, I should like to know before I agree to marry you that there could at least be a small amount of attraction between us beyond the friendship we have always shared. So, I must kiss you." And without allowing her time to think or argue, he did just that.

He had expected it to be pleasant, but he had not expected to have to fight to keep his arms from drawing her near. Nor had he expected to find it so very difficult to break away from her. In fact, he found he needed a moment after ending the kiss before he was certain his voice would be even close to normal.

He stood and straightened his coat before offering her his hand. "I shall have Mr. Harker call the banns," he said. "We marry in three weeks."

Chapter 2

The rain had only started to fall lightly as the parishioners began to file out of the small church in Kympton. The migration of people from pew to door was a slow one as each took a moment to comment on Mr. Dobney's sermon and to congratulate him on his upcoming marriage.

Rather than joining the numbers that lined the aisle, Lucy remained seated near the front of the church but turned so that she might watch the man she would soon call husband. He smiled and laughed. He ruffled the hair of children and shook the hands of their fathers. He had always greeted people with such ease and welcome — as if he had always known them.

She rested an elbow on the back of the pew and her head lightly on her hand as she watched him nod his head and tap his lip with a finger before replying to Mr. Evans. She knew from the actions that he was giving some bit of advice, for he never did so without at least a moment's thought. Even when they were children, he had been the one to whom the others had looked to for guidance, and he had provided it without ever making one of them feel as if they were lacking in any way.

She smiled as he leaned his tall frame down to speak closely into Mrs. Walcroft's ear. Others might have raised their voice to talk to the woman, but he never did. Philip was cautious not to injure the dignity of others, no matter their age or frailties. It was something she had always admired about him; however, not all had found the trait admirable. In fact, there were those who, at one time, had thought it a weakness and had teased Philip relentlessly.

It was not the only thing about which Philip had been teased. He had been gangly as a young man. His arms and legs seemed to grow rapidly, much more rapidly than his ability to use them with grace and dignity. He had also been rather skinny until he had gone away to college. However, during those years, his body had finally righted itself. He had not added another inch to his height, and he was no longer skinny.

She ducked her head as she felt a bit of colour creeping into cheeks when she realized just how fine he now appeared to her. He was still taller than most, but his clothes no longer hung on him. She turned her mind away from admiring how his jacket now stretched across his back and wrapped snuggly around arms that were well-muscled and strong.

Lucy rested a gloved finger on her lips. She had chosen

him for his admirable character, but since that kiss two days ago...

She swallowed and rose from her seat. This was not the place to be contemplating fine figures or kisses. However, she could not resist taking one more look at Philip before she ducked out the side door.

She pulled her wrap about her and dashed to stand under a well-leaved tree. She leaned against the tree and closed her eyes, filling her lungs with air that was washed clean by the falling rain. Expelling it, she opened her eyes and searched for things, other than Philip and that kiss, with which to occupy her thoughts. She was certain it was quite improper for her to have enjoyed it so. Indeed, in the moments when she was not applying herself to one task or another, it had often crept into her mind.

She gave herself a little shake and began watching the horses and carriages travelling along the road and the people who hurried along on foot. Despite the inclement weather, the church had been full. Even Philip's patron had been in attendance today, but knowing what day it was, she had expected him to be there. He never missed his mother's birthday. He had returned from town just yesterday, according to the ladies who had been sitting behind her during the service.

Her eyes wandered across the churchyard. Ah, there he was, kneeling on the damp ground, brushing away whatever traces of dirt might have accumulated on his mother's name. She understood his need to be there. Once a year, she, too, would visit her mother's grave, flowers in hand, words of love and thankfulness on her lips. She sighed. She would be making that journey twice a year now.

"Lucy," Philip said as he approached, "why are you standing out here in the rain? You will catch a chill."

Lucy glanced at Philip and gave him a small smile. "I felt a need for some air, and I knew you would not be long. Is Mr. Harker ready?"

Philip smiled and shook his head. "But he will be soon. He only had two more people with whom he wished to speak."

"So, a quarter hour then?" Lucy asked with a laugh. Mr. Harker was not known for the brevity of his conversations.

"If we are so fortunate," said Philip. He offered her his arm and nodded toward the churchyard. "Do you wish to visit your father?"

She smiled up at him and nodded as she wound her arm through his, stepping in close so that the umbrella might shield them both from the majority of the rain that was now steadily falling.

A picture of strolling just like this after every service formed unbidden in his mind and a sense of peace and comfort washed over him. He shook his head. His reaction to her continued to amaze him. He had definitely felt a certain amount of friendship with her for many years. Her loyalty, as well as her honesty, had always impressed him.

It was something he had treasured about his friendship with her. In fact, he had treasured it so much that she, though she did not know it, had been one of the few people he had ever asked for advice. Then, when she had proposed the idea of marriage, he had felt a certain amount of duty to her — a responsibility to see her safe and well-cared-for — much as he had when they were young and his mother had assigned him to look out for Mary Ellen and Lucy. But then, he had kissed her, and that had set off a full range of new and wholly unexpected emotions. And now, with her here walking next to him...

"Is something troubling you?" They stood before her father's grave, but instead of leaving his arm and attending to whatever bit of information she wished to speak to her father, she stood, holding his arm firmly and looking up at him in concern. "You look rather pensive and perhaps a bit puzzled."

"I was just thinking about our future," he said looking down at her.

"And it makes you draw your brows together and frown?"

He laughed lightly. "I do that when I am thinking especially hard. It does not mean the topic of consideration is unpleasant." He was relieved to see her expression soften.

"And how do you see the future, Mr. Dob — Philip?" she corrected as he raised a brow at her.

He patted her arm and a joyous smile lit his face. "Happy, Lucy. Very, very happy."

Lucy gave Philip's arm a squeeze before releasing it. "I believe you are right. We will be happy," she said before turning to her father's grave.

"Mr. Dobney," Lucy heard a gentleman calling to Philip as she spoke softly to her father telling him that the first of the banns had been read that morning and assuring him that her future would be secure and happy.

"Mr. Darcy," Philip greeted the gentleman who had called to him. "It was a pleasure to have you amongst the faces in church today. I trust you are well?"

"I am well."

"And your sister? Does she still find school a challenge?" Philip remembered the shy young girl who had peeked out from behind curtains and doors when he had visited his friend at Pemberley.

Darcy sighed. "She does. My cousin and I are considering removing her from school."

Philip cocked his head to the side and looked carefully at his friend, who had in the last three years since his father's death grown so much more serious than he had even been as a child. The responsibility of an estate as grand as Pemberley and the guardianship of a younger sister must be an immense weight to carry.

"It might be for the best," he said. "Individual instruction can be most beneficial to some, and as long as you find her a proper companion, she may do very well. Of course, one can never be certain."

Darcy nodded a greeting to Lucy as she came to stand at Philip's side. "No, my friend, nothing is ever certain."

"Uncertainty does not have to be something to dread," said Lucy, "though it does make one feel ill at ease. I find a plan the best remedy for the feeling."

Darcy could not help but smile at her comments. She had always been the most positive of his acquaintances. "And," he cocked a brow, "Philip here is part of your plan?"

Lucy laughed and wrapped her arm around Philip's. "He is now."

"Now?"

Lucy's eyes flicked quickly to her father's grave. "My plans to spend some time in finding a suitable match were altered, so the process had to be hastened."

"I was sorry to hear of your father's passing," Darcy said.

"Thank you." Lucy looked at Philip. "Would this conversation not be much better if we were out of the rain and perhaps had a cup of tea or a meal in front of us?"

Philip chuckled at her gentle way of making a suggestion. "I believe you are correct. Mr. Darcy, would you care to join us for our repast? I believe Mr. Harker will be ready to leave soon."

Lucy waited long enough to get Darcy's acceptance before telling Philip she would inform Mr. Harker.

"A marriage of convenience?" asked Darcy as he watched Lucy walking toward the church.

Philip nodded. "Her uncle offered to take her if she was not married in two months, and you know what he is like. I would not wish to subject any young lady to his care." He knew Darcy was familiar with Angus Tolson's proclivities. "So, when she presented the idea of marriage, I could not refuse."

Darcy studied the look on his friend's face. "You do not seem displeased with the idea. In fact, I am not sure I have ever seen you look so at ease."

Philip shrugged slightly. "I admit there is a certain amount of peace that has taken up residence in my heart knowing that one aspect of my future is secured."

Darcy shook his head. "No, there must be more to it. I have seen many who have married for convenience, and it is rare to find one who looks as you do."

"Perhaps it is because she has always been my friend," Philip suggested. "I know her. Many who marry do not truly know each other — at least, not as I know her."

"Perhaps," agreed Darcy, though his tone spoke of his disbelief. However, their discussion of Lucy was soon to come to an end, for the very lady was presently assisting Mr. Harker toward where they stood and the carriage waited. "She will make a fine parson's wife."

"Yes, I know," said Philip as a strange feeling of pride filled him. "She told me she would." He reached into his pocket. "She had a list." He handed the list to Darcy. "Make sure I get that back, and please, do not let her know I have given it to you. I am sure she would not mind your seeing it since we are all such good friends, but I would rather not find out I am wrong."

Darcy chuckled and slipped the paper into his pocket as Philip left him to assist Mr. Harker and Lucy into the carriage.

Chapter 3

Darcy slipped the letter he had been given to read back to Philip as they entered the sitting room at the parsonage. "She was always the brightest among us," he said softly. "You cannot fault her logic."

Philip watched Lucy begin to pour the tea and smiled. "I believe, she will do quite nicely," he agreed.

"Even better than that," muttered Mr. Harker as he bumped his way past Philip. The gentleman's eyesight might nearly be gone, but his hearing was still sharp. "It will be pleasant to have her come visit me once I am settled into my cottage."

"You know you are welcome to stay with us," said Philip.

"Oh, I know," said Mr. Harker with a smile and a flick of his brow, "but you will be grateful for your privacy, I assure you."

Darcy chuckled as his friend's face grew red.

"And I," continued Mr. Harker, "will be glad for the

quiet. Shepherding a flock is a noisy business. I shall enjoy my ease."

"You will wish for company soon enough," said Darcy.

"Bah," Mr. Harker took his seat. "They'll not leave me alone. I shall have company aplenty."

"More than you would wish for," agreed Philip. "There are those in Kympton who will make it their duty to see you entertained and well-fed. Mrs. Walcroft was inquiring about you today."

"Mrs. Walcroft, Mrs. Blakely, Mrs. Evans," grumbled Mr. Harker as Lucy placed his tea on the table next to him before touching his hand and telling him where the cup was.

"It is reassuring to know you will not be lonely," said Darcy with a chuckle.

Mr. Harker smiled and lifted his cup of tea. "Mrs. Evans does make a delicious mincemeat pie."

"Like I said," commented Philip as he brushed past Lucy and took a seat, "you will be well-fed."

"Mr. Darcy." Lucy handed him a cup of tea.

"Thank you, Miss Tolson." He settled into a comfortable chair in the sitting room of the parsonage. He had spent many hours right here conversing with Mr. Harker. It was a friendship that had developed after his mother had died and had continued to grow over the years. His friendship with Mr. Harker had been invaluable when Darcy's father had fallen ill and he had found himself facing the responsibilities of not only an estate but those of caring for his younger sister. Mr. Harker sat now where he had sat on each of those visits, in a chair tucked away in the corner just to his left. Darcy took a sip of his tea. "When will your uncle be coming?"

The cup Lucy held clattered just slightly. The thought of his return made her nerves jump and quiver. "He will be here in just over a month's time. He wishes to have an accounting of all the items in the house before the new tenants take up residency." She knew that many of the items would be packed up and taken back to town and sold to cover debts. She had already seen to the moving of the pieces left to her by her mother, so that they would not go missing.

"He will not be returning to stay?" Darcy was not at all surprised, nor was he disappointed by the information. To own the truth, he was rather pleased.

"My uncle prefers town, and I prefer him to remain in town," said Lucy, passing a cup to Philip before filling one for herself.

"As do many," muttered Mr. Harker.

"Thankfully," continued Lucy as she took a seat next to Mrs. Barnes, more commonly known as her Aunt Tess, "he will not arrive before Mr. Dobney and I have wed."

Darcy cocked his head to one side. "You would expect him to cause trouble?"

Lucy sat her cup on the side table and folded her hands

in her lap. She dared not hold a cup of hot tea while discussing her uncle, for she was sure she would slosh at least some if not all of it on her clothes. To say she was not fond of her uncle was an understatement. To say she feared him was much closer to the truth. "Only if he is in need of money, which he nearly always is."

Darcy also put his cup aside. "I have met many like him." He turned the handle of the cup away from himself and back again. There was no need for the motion other than to give his hand something to do and his eyes something on which to focus other than those looking at him now. There was a topic he knew he must broach and of which both Mr. Harker and Mr. Dobney needed to be aware. However, the subject was not one that was easily canvassed. "I was visited by such a one just yesterday."

"Wickham?" asked Philip softly. In the whole of their acquaintance, there were few who caused Darcy to fidget with uneasiness as he was now. George Wickham was very adept at making Darcy uneasy. He was known for his purposeful gibes at Darcy, as well as his playing at causing trouble for him. How Darcy had managed to tolerate the young fool for as long as he had — even if it was merely for the sake of his father — had always astounded Philip.

"Did he ask about the living?" There was no doubt in Philip's mind as to what that meeting had been about. Philip knew the details of Darcy's father's will and the arrangement that had been made with Wickham when he had declined the living in favour of a monetary settlement, for Darcy had discussed them with Philip before allowing him to accept the living as his own. There was an understandable uneasiness even then in Darcy's manners. They both knew that Wickham would one day challenge the arrangement and plead how the elder Mr. Darcy's will had not been kept.

"He did, and I refused to hear of it, of course." Darcy looked out the window. "He claims his circumstances are dire, and I have no doubt they are."

"He is like my uncle," said Lucy, rising to gather the cups. Her hands often felt the need to be busy when her mind was disquieted. "He will apply to you again and again. And then, when he is unsuccessful, he will look for another method of gaining what he wants." Her voice grew more panicked with each successive word, and her hands trembled, causing the cups to clatter.

Phillip, who was near her, reached out, steadied them, and then took them from her. She was not one to be easily rattled. She had listed that trait as one of her qualifications for marrying him, and so her state of agitation spoke to him of some awful truth that lay hidden.

Aunt Tess, who had lived with and helped care for Lucy for years, stood and wrapped an arm around her niece's shoulders. "He may be like your uncle, but he is not your uncle. We will be well. You shall marry Mr. Dobney, and we shall be well." She guided Lucy back to the settee they had been sharing. Taking her seat, she took Lucy's hand in both of hers. "It is time we spoke of it," she said gently to Lucy, who swallowed and nodded her consent.

"As you know," said Aunt Tess, turning toward Philip and Darcy, "I came to live with Lucy and her parents six years ago. My husband had left me with the means to establish a place of my own should I wish it, but I preferred to be surrounded by those I love." She patted Lucy's hand affectionately. "The decision, I believe, was providential, for shortly after I arrived, Lucy's mother was injured while riding." She sighed slightly. "She never fully recovered. Her constitution was weakened. She tired easily and became readily susceptible to illness, taking to her bed regularly until finally she succumbed completely and was no more."

Philip watched Lucy chew the corner of her lip and knew that she was battling the emotions that recounting such events must necessarily arouse.

"Shortly thereafter," continued Aunt Tess, "my youngest brother appeared, insisting that he needed help. He had lost money, he said, in a speculation," she raised an eyebrow indicating she did not believe the explanation, "He, of course, had debts that needed repayment. The money lost was money which Simon had previously given Angus to cover another pressing debt. Simon was rightfully furious and refused Angus the money. No matter how Angus pleaded, Simon held firm. It was a trying few days. The sound of raised voices was common. We were all relieved when Angus finally packed his bags and mounted his horse."

"But he had not truly left," said Lucy with a quick glance at her aunt. "A week later, he crept into the house and found my aunt in her chamber. I was in her dressing room."

Aunt Tess's hand rested on Lucy's knee, rubbing it just slightly. "Angus knew that I was not without means, but he also knew that I would not part with those means easily."

Philip noted how tightly Lucy's hands were clasped in her lap and how often she drew in a deep breath as if needing to fortify herself. Again, just as it had when she had spoken to him so fearfully in the churchyard, his chest constricted, and his heart longed so intensely to see her protected that it hurt.

"I tried to stay quietly hidden in the dressing room," Lucy's voice was apologetic, "but I bumped a brush, and when it clattered to the floor, he found me."

Aunt Tess's arm wrapped around Lucy's shoulders once again. "Lucy had to wear long sleeves for a month to hide the marks his hands made when he grabbed her." She smiled sadly at her niece. "But that was not the worst of it."

Lucy shook her head, wishing for the story to stop, and her aunt, seeing her distress, said no more. The room fell silent for a moment until Lucy, gathering her courage, continued the tale.

"He said the man to whom he owed the debt would gladly accept a young and eager bride in place of the money." She closed her eyes and shook her head again; perhaps she did not have the courage to tell it all. "He then enumerated what exactly he expected the man would appreciate about my person." Even now, she could feel his hands touching her as he spoke of it. She could smell the stench of alcohol as he spoke near her ear, and her stomach twisted and turned with revulsion just as it had then.

"I could not allow that, of course," said Aunt Tess, drawing Lucy as close as possible, "so I gave him what he wanted."

"And you fear that Wickham will attempt to hurt you to get what he wants?" asked Philip, looking intently at Lucy. He longed to be where her aunt was now, with his arms around her and her head on his shoulder, providing comfort and a feeling of security.

Lucy lifted one shoulder and let it drop. "As silly as it sounds, I do, and if not me, then one of you. Men like my uncle do not admit defeat easily."

"I will not allow it," said Philip, standing and pacing the room. His emotions could no longer be contained without some escape of movement.

"Nor will I," said Mr. Harker and Darcy nearly as one.

The vehemence in Philip's voice surprised Darcy. His

friend had always been gentle and peaceable. He had rarely shown any sort of anger, and only in instances when those he cared for deeply, such as his sister or his brother, had been threatened. Despite the seriousness of the moment, Darcy found himself smiling as he watched Philip pace the room. No matter how much his friend insisted that he was marrying Lucy out of convenience or some sense of duty, Darcy suspected that Philip had actually fallen in love with the woman who was soon to be his wife.

Chapter 4

The following morning, having already made her selections, Lucy stepped outside the milliner's shop to wait for her aunt. A soft, cool breeze blew, tugging gently at her bonnet. She turned her face to the sun. It was pleasant to feel its warmth on her cheeks for the few brief moments she allowed them to be tilted upward. She would like nothing better than to remove her bonnet and drink in the sunshine, but her skin was fair, and where others would turn brown from the sun, she only turned painfully red. She glanced through the shop window and watched as the milliner's assistant showed her aunt ribbons and lace. She smiled. Her aunt was never without an exquisitely decorated cap.

"Miss Tolson."

Lucy heart skipped a beat at the voice. Slowly, she turned to face the speaker. "Mr. Wickham," she said in greeting, with a quick curtsey and a nervous glance toward the shop.

"It is a fine day for shopping, is it not?" He shoved the

small package he was carrying into the pocket of his great coat. "The sun is warm, the breeze is cool, and the shops are filled with smiling faces."

"Indeed, it is a lovely day, Mr. Wickham. My aunt is just finishing placing an order for a new bonnet," Lucy took a step toward the door to the shop. Although he wore a friendly expression, she knew better than to trust that there was anything akin to friendship behind his greeting. He had always been able to convince people of his sincerity with his flowery word and pleasant smile, but she had seen his true character displayed more than once while they were growing up. She also knew that he had been unsuccessful in his meeting with Mr. Darcy, which meant he would be looking for a new slant, a new approach, to gaining that which he desired.

"I was sorry to hear of your father's passing." Wickham stepped towards her. His features drooped with feigned grief, and his shoulders sagged just a bit. "He was a good man from all accounts."

"He was," agreed Lucy, watching him warily. His posture shifted just slightly. His shoulders rose and his countenance brightened, though Lucy was not certain if it would be more accurate to say he smiled with restrained delight or just mere cunning.

"I also understand that you are to marry. I believe the younger Mr. Dobney is the lucky fellow, is he not?"

Lucy glanced again toward the shop. Her Heart was

beginning to beat more rapidly the longer she stood here talking to him, and her stomach began to twist into a knot. She wished desperately for her aunt to conclude her business and step outside. "He is," she said.

"A rather sudden engagement, I hear." An eyebrow flicked upwards as he smirked at her.

Lucy heard the hidden implication in his tone and read it in his expression. She wished to pull her pelisse more tightly about herself and turn away from his roaming eyes. "You have been busy catching up on all the news, have you not?" she said somewhat sharply.

He chuckled and allowed his eyes to roam her figure once again. "One hears things," he said as he took his watch from his pocket. "Well, I must be off, or I shall be late." He took two steps away before turning back with a most evil smile on his face. "Do you wish me to give a greeting to your uncle?"

Panic gripped Lucy's heart. The world felt as if it was shaking, causing her to sway and struggle to keep her balance. "My...my...uncle?" she eventually forced out the words.

Wickham stepped closer once again and placed one hand on her elbow to steady her while he placed his other hand inappropriately low on her back. "Well, Tolson told me his arrival would come as a shock to you, but I had not expected you to nearly swoon."

She pulled her arm away from him and took a step forward. "I did not almost swoon," she snapped. "I was merely surprised that you know my uncle so well."

He shrugged. "If you say so, but I suppose any lady who wished to pass herself off as chaste enough to be a parson's wife would be worried to the point of swooning if she knew the stories that could be told about her."

She wished to end this conversation and run to her aunt, who was still inside the shop, but her feet were rooted to the spot where she stood. Her eyebrows furrowed, and she shook her head. "There are no stories," she said.

He shrugged once more. "If you say so."

"I do say so. There are no stories."

He laughed. "Oh, Miss Tolson, there are stories." He picked at a piece of lint on the jacket of his coat. "I am sure an arrangement can be reached where you can continue to be thought of as a paragon of virtue."

"An arrangement?" She remembered the same word being used by her uncle when he had discussed her becoming the young bride of the man to whom he owed money. The pieces were beginning to fall into place in her mind. Although still wary and fearful, she was becoming increasingly angry at Wickham's hints of knowing some secret. Pushing her fear to the side, she drew a fortifying breath and asked the question that would confirm her suspicions about her uncle and Mr. Wickham being associates. "Mr. Wickham, exactly how do you know my uncle?"

Again, he shrugged. "I grew up here. Everyone knows your uncle."

She shook her head. "No, he left when I was quite young, and you are not that much older than I am. You would not have been old enough to have formed such an intimate acquaintance before he left." She cocked her head to the side and studied Wickham's face. His eyes shifted uneasily under her scrutiny. "You have met him since."

"Very well," admitted Wickham. "We have been friends and business associates for just over a year." He took a step closer to her, and any false pretense of friendliness left his features. "But, I assure you, there are tales that can be told. You would do well to be more receptive to his offer when he visits you this time."

Dread settled in Lucy's stomach, but she dared not acknowledge it. He had seen her fearful reaction once; to offer him a second glimpse of the terror her uncle brought to her heart was not something she was willing to do. "Tell him," she said as calmly as she was able, "that he may call for tea tomorrow. I am sure he is anxious to see that the estate is in order and ready for its transfer. You may assure him that it is." The door to the milliner's shop creaked behind her. "Good day, Mr. Wickham." She bobbed a quick curtsey and turned toward her aunt, who was just exiting the store.

"To whom were you speaking?" asked Aunt Tess as she reached Lucy's side.

Lucy let out a shuddering breath, finally releasing some of the fear that had gripped her. "It was Mr. Wickham."

"What did he say to you?" Aunt Tess took Lucy by the arm and began hurrying her in the direction of the parsonage, which was much closer than her home.

Lucy felt decidedly weak, and she knew she was trembling.

"He asked if there was a message I wished for him to give to my uncle."

Aunt Tess's grip on Lucy's arm tightened and her pace increased. "Your uncle is here?"

Lucy shrugged. "I am not certain, but Mr. Wickham made it sound as if he is."

She and her aunt moved further to the side of the lane as a barouche approached, but instead of passing as they had expected it would, it came to a stop next to them.

"Miss Tolson, Mrs. Barnes," Philip called to them. "Could we give you a ride?"

Aunt Tess eagerly accepted the offer, and soon the two ladies were seated in the carriage with Darcy and Philip. "We were on our way to the parsonage," she explained as the horses began walking. "I was unsure that Lucy would make the full journey home. She had a bit of a fright."

"You are unwell?" Philip asked.

Lucy ducked her head and clasped her hands tightly in her lap. His tone was so serious, so filled with concern.

"I had a small conversation with Mr. Wickham."

"Wickham?" asked Darcy.

Lucy gave him a weak smile and nodded head. "He mentioned my uncle was here."

Shock suffused Darcy's face. "Your uncle and Wickham are acquaintances?"

"Business associates, according to Mr. Wickham, which," she took a breath and blew it out, "means they are both in need of money. I would venture to guess that Mr. Wickham, since he has already petitioned you for the living, is in debt to my uncle, and my uncle is in debt to someone else." She turned to Aunt Tess. "He said I should be more receptive to my uncle's offer this time when he calls on me. He knows of what happened and has threatened to use it to tarnish my reputation."

Philip looked at her in confusion. "How could a tale about a man attempting to force you into marriage harm your reputation?"

Aunt Tess had wrapped an arm around Lucy. "Lucy was preparing for bed when he visited last time. She was not dressed to receive visitors and was less dressed when he left, for he tore her clothes from her as he spoke of her particularly attractive attributes. She was not violated in any other way than being seen disrobed and, of course, touched as he removed her clothing. She is still as virtuous as any maiden, but her uncle is not above lying."

Lucy's face burned crimson, and she dared not look at either gentleman in the carriage.

Philip reached across the carriage to take her hand. "What can I do to protect you?"

What he wished to do was pull her into his arms and ride away with her to some place where her uncle was not. Her peculiar effect on his feelings once again surprised him.

Lucy peeked up at him. There was no judgment in his eyes, only concern. "I do not know," she whispered.

"We must not return home," said Aunt Tess.

"Pemberley," said Darcy. "You must come to Pemberley." He laid a hand on Philip's shoulder. "You and I and a stout footman or two shall spend the night at Willow Hall in case Lucy's uncle decides to visit in the same manner he did last time. I believe Mr. Harker should join the ladies at Pemberley."

"I have told Mr. Wickham that my uncle may call on me tomorrow for tea to inspect the estate and see that all is in order for the transfer to new tenants," said Lucy.

"Then it is most imperative that you stay at Pemberley, and we keep watch over Willow Hall. If he is as desperate as I know Wickham is, your uncle may try to alter things so that he can blame you. If he can make you appear to be an unacceptable choice for Mr. Dobney; then you will have no option but to return to his home with him." Darcy rubbed his chin. "How exactly Wickham and his request for the living fit into this scheme I do not know."

Lucy squeezed Philip's hand, which still held hers. "I believe I know," she said softly. "Mr. Wickham must owe him a substantial amount of money."

"But how will ruining you help Wickham?" asked Philip.

"If he can discredit me in the eyes of the village, he can certainly do the same to you. Who would wish for or listen to a minister who has been taken in by a fallen woman? Indeed, who would respect a man who preaches purity when he himself has rushed into a marriage because of a lack of restraint?"

"But we are not marrying for that reason," protested Philip.

"No, we are not, but it is what Mr. Wickham implied."

Philip's eyes grew wide and then narrowed with anger.

"She is right," said Darcy gravely. "Tolson may not be readily believed, but we all know how convincing Wickham can be."

"So what do we do?" asked Philip.

"The ladies and Mr. Harker will go to Pemberley, and we will stay at Willow Hall as planned. Perhaps, if we are fortunate, we can stop them before they have begun."

Aunt Tess agreed with the plan but added. "I know that none of you approve of gossip, and neither do I, of course;

however, a word of caution to the staff at Willow Hall about Lucy's uncle with a suggestion of his debauchery would not be out of order."

Darcy smiled. "And we know that servants do not always keep all tales to themselves."

"Especially when they are not instructed to," said Aunt Tess, returning Darcy's smile and tapping her nose.

"Very good," said Darcy. "Ladies to Pemberley, gents to Willow Hall, and tales to those who will carry them."

Chapter 5

Lucy looked around her room while mentally ticking off the items she had put in her bag and attempting to ensure she had not forgotten anything that she would need for her stay at Pemberley. Her eyes came to rest on the book next to her bed. "Of course," she said. Picking up the book, she turned it over in her hands and ran her finger along the blue ribbon that held her place.

> *He prayeth best who loveth best,*
>
> *All things both great and small:*
>
> *For the dear God, who loveth us,*
>
> *He made and loveth all,*[1]

She quoted the familiar lines as she tucked the book under her clothes in her bag. It was a book she had read many times, a book which had been a gift from her father

1. (from THE RIME OF THE ANCYENT MARINERE, IN SEVEN PARTS, by Samuel Taylor Coleridge)

to her mother, a book that she had heard her father read to her mother as they sat before the fire in the evenings. And it was the book she had read while her father had breathed his last. She dabbed at the corners of her eyes. It was a book with which she would never part. The memories attached to it were greater even than the wonderful words contained within it.

"Miss?" A maid stood at the door. "There is a letter for you."

"A letter?" She took the letter from the maid. "I did not heard a rider." There had been no crunching of the gravel on the drive or banging on the door. Both were things she would have heard from her room since it was situated facing the front of the house.

The maid wrung her hands nervously. "There was no rider, miss. Only a man in gentlemen's clothing at the kitchen door." Her voice was soft, and she peeked down the hall behind her. "I weren't supposed to tell you, miss."

The letter trembled slightly in Lucy's hand, so she tucked it into her pocket. She fought to keep her voice steady as she questioned the maid. "Do you know where my aunt is?"

"Yes, miss. She is in the sitting room with the gentlemen. Jonathan is waiting to take her bag to the carriage when he takes yours." The maid dipped a small curtsey and turned to leave.

"Margaret," Lucy called to the maid before she could

scoot away. "This man." She held up the letter. "Is he gone?"

"I do not know, miss. I did not tarry when he told me to be quick. I feared he might hit me if I did."

Lucy's brows rose, but she dismissed the maid with the instructions that her bag was now ready for Jonathan to take to the carriage. Taking the letter from her pocket, she turned it over in her hands so that she could see the seal. There was the distinctive *T* in the wax. It was, she suspected, from her uncle. She shook her head at his cunningness. He had selected a maid who had not been in their employ long enough to know his identity.

She crossed to her window and looked out, even though she did not expect to see him since he had made his delivery at the back of the house. The carriage waited in front of the house, and beyond a footman and a coachman. There was no one in front of the house.

"Are you not going to read it?"

Lucy froze at the sound of her uncle's voice.

"Are you not going to read it?" Lucy's uncle repeated.

Lucy closed her eyes briefly and took a steadying breath before turning around to face him. "I shall read it. Just not now." She slipped the letter back into her pocket. "I was on my way to visit with friends, and they are waiting. I shall not keep them waiting." She was not sure her legs would carry her the full way or that passing so close to him to leave the room was a wise choice, but she was certain she did not wish to remain in this room with him.

"I think," he said as he nudged her bedroom door closed with his foot, "that you should read it now. I am rather impatient for an answer."

"If you are so impatient for an answer, why do you not just make your request and be done? I do not see why you bothered to take the time to write a message if you had every intention of speaking to me in person." Lucy hoped that the trembling she felt was not visible to him. She knew she must act confident even if she did not feel it. "Jonathan is to arrive soon to collect my bag, and my aunt and my friends will wonder when I do not appear in the sitting room soon."

He stepped closer to her and clucked his tongue. "Your manners are not at all those of a well-bred lady and certainly not the sort that would do honour to a parson." He took a moment to admire her features. "Your beauty is not that of which the poets write, but I must say you are very womanly. I still have at least one associate who would be pleased to have you." He took one step closer. "You have not forgotten my previous offer, have you?"

Lucy fought the urge to wrap her arms around herself and hide from his gaze. "My friends are waiting, Uncle."

"Ah, yes, your parson and Darcy. One who holds a position that should be another's and the other, the lying, thief who gave it him." He crossed to her bed and began to open her bag. "You really should seek better friends." He pulled out a chemise and stuffed it inside his coat.

"What are you doing?" Lucy had crossed the room when he had begun to open her bag and now she snatched it from him.

"Read my message, my dear." He smiled wickedly at her as he tugged the bag out of her hands. "I would like to have my answer now, but since you will not obey me and read that letter as a good girl should, I will be forced to wait until tomorrow." He pulled the book of poetry from the bag and opening it, tore out one page. "Disobedience must be punished. This was your mother's book, was it not?"

"How did you know?"

He smiled that wicked grin again. "There is much you would be surprised that I know." He tucked the torn page into her bag and the book into his coat. "One page every hour until I have my answer, Lucy. And if you speak of the contents of that letter to anyone. I will consign the entire book to the flames and that will merely be the beginning of your punishment." He gave a bow and slipped out the door.

Shaking, Lucy sat on the bed and took out the letter.

I have two "requests" to make of you, my dear niece.

First, I have need of your mother's necklace — the one with the golden leaves. Leave it at her grave.

Her hand rested on her heart. First, he took her mother's book, and now, he wished to steal her mother's necklace? She was not certain she wished to know what the second request was, yet she read on.

Second, I have need of the living which your betrothed now has. A friend is in need of an income. Please do persuade your parson that he should seek another position. It would do me great pain to have to make your soiled state known to the public, but I will if need be.

Ah, you are wondering at how I know of these things?
She was.

I have in my possession a certain garment of yours which is worn close to the body.
She gasped. That was why he took her chemise! Horror washed over her as she read his next words.

I believe you left it as a token of your affection the last time you visited your lover. And if I believe it, so will others.
He would ruin her reputation and Philip's right along with it.

Convince him, and you shall be married as planned.

There are yet two reading of the banns, are there not?
Lucy let the letter fall into her lap as she pulled out the torn page and read some of what was written there. She

needed something — anything — with which to push his words from her mind and keep her tears from falling.

Farewell, farewell! but this I tell

To thee, thou wedding guest!

He prayeth well who loveth well

Both man and bird and beast.

He prayeth best who loveth best,

All things both great and small:

For the dear God, who loveth us,

He made and loveth all.

The Marinere, whose eye is bright,

Whose beard with age is hoar,

Is gone; and now the wedding-guest

Turn'd from the bridegroom's door.

He went, like one that hath been stunn'd

And is of sense forlorn:

A sadder and a wiser man

He rose the morrow morn.[2]

Lucy folded the poem with great care and tucked it between her clothing. She felt a great deal like the wedding guest — stunned, forlorn, and grieved. She went to the wardrobe and took out another chemise. She ran her fingers over the delicate flowers she had embroidered on the neckline before tucking the garment into her bag. Her mother had taught her to do that stitch and had insisted that every undergarment have at least one flower on it. For, her mother had explained, "A secret bit of beauty, hidden away such as this, has the ability to make the wearer feel that beauty and carry herself with grace and poise."

And Lucy had obeyed. Every chemise and every petticoat was adorned with those flowers. It would be a tell-tale sign that the chemise her uncle had stolen was hers. The lying scoundrel! She snatched his letter from the bed, crumpled it and placed it between the wood in the fireplace so that it might be burned when the next fire was lit.

Then, she returned to the wardrobe and took out a handkerchief. She placed it on the bed and slipped the necklace from around her neck. She folded the cloth around the necklace and, taking a ribbon, tied it securely.

"Sarah," she called from her doorway to a maid who was just down the hall. "I need you to do something for me today." She placed the necklace in Sarah's hand. "This

2. *(Also from THE RIME OF THE ANCYENT MARINERE, IN SEVEN PARTS, by Samuel Taylor Coleridge)*

must be left at my mother's grave as soon as can be. It is something I had promised to lend a friend, and my friend will be looking for it." She bit her lip. The falsehood hung in the air, taunting her, tempting her to snatch it back and correct her words, but with her mother's book in her uncle's possession, along with her chemise, she dared not speak the truth.

"Today? At your mother's grave?" asked Sarah.

"Yes, immediately, if you would."

Sarah's brows drew together slightly as if she questioned such an unusual request, but she obediently bobbed her head and left with the necklace.

Lucy looked around the room. She did not know what she intended to do about the living, but she hoped that the necklace would provide her with some time to consider it.

"Are you ready?"

Lucy jumped at her aunt's words. Her hand flew to her throat, and she gasped.

"Are you well?" asked Aunt Tess, coming to her side. "You do look a bit pale."

"I am well." Lucy smiled at her aunt. "I was merely running through a list in my mind and did not hear you approach."

Aunt Tess raised a brow in disbelief and placed an arm around Lucy's shoulders, then quickly pressed the back of her hand against first Lucy's cheek and then her forehead. "You are shaking. Come. We must get you to Pemberley and see if Mrs. Reynolds will be so kind as to have the cook make you some broth." She clucked her tongue and shook her head. "You never admit to being unwell until it is far too late. This time, you shall be made well before your body has determined it is indeed ill."

"I am well," insisted Lucy. "I find today to be a bit cool and with no fire in the grate, I must shiver to stay warm."

"You shall still have broth, tea, and toast and retire early," said her aunt. "I shall not see you ill due to a chill."

Lucy sighed. There was no way to convince her aunt of her good health other than to tell her of the letter, and that was not something she was prepared to do just yet. Perhaps after she had had some time to consider what could be done, then she would tell her aunt. And so, she allowed her aunt to bundle her in an extra wrap and lead her from the room. It could not be helped; she would just have to allow her aunt to care for her as if she had taken a chill.

Chapter 6

Philip and Darcy remained for a time in the sitting room after the ladies and Mr. Harker had left Willow Hall. Darcy drummed his fingers on the arm of the chair and stared into the fire while Philip paced the room.

Finally, Philip broke the silence. "She was not well. Something is amiss."

Darcy nodded. He, too, had noted the paleness of Lucy's complexion and the way her eyes had not once sought his or Philip's. It was unlike her, but then she had been quite unlike herself ever since she had heard of Wickham's seeking the living.

To be honest, after listening to the tale her aunt told yesterday and added to today, he did not fault her for her fear. How any man, let alone one who was a close relative, could treat a young girl so contemptibly was beyond him! "This business with her uncle is very unsettling."

Philip dropped into the chair across from his friend. "That it is, but I cannot help feeling as if there is something more." He leaned back and looked up at the ceiling.

"She was not so distressed earlier when we arrived so the ladies could collect their things."

Again, Darcy nodded his agreement. "That is true. However, abandoning your home because you fear for your safety while in it is naturally distressing."

Philip sighed and lapsed into silence. He could not imagine fearing for his safety within his own home. And he knew that for Lucy the fear lived in more than the imaginings of a wary woman. She was not prone to fits of nerves. No, this fear got its breath and strength from the fact that her safety had been compromised in her very home by her relation all those years ago. He sat up suddenly as a thought occurred to him. "Darcy? In Lucy's story about her uncle, how did her uncle enter her house undetected? Surely, he did not enter through the front door."

"The servant's entry? A window?" Darcy suggested.

Philip was on his feet once again. "We shall have to post a man at the servant's door."

"One of mine," said Darcy. "They are loyal to me. As much as I do not like to think it, there could be a servant here who might be easily persuaded to assist Tolson. I do not know Lucy's staff as I know my own."

Philip nodded. "I should like to see to the locking of all the windows myself. Do you care to accompany me?"

Darcy stood and straightened his coat. "As soon as I appoint someone to watch the servant's entry and perhaps another to stand guard in the hall. There is nothing to stop someone from unlocking a window after we have secured it."

"The upstairs hall should also have a man stationed in it."

It was a suggestion with which Darcy agreed, and stepping into the hall, he found one of his men. Quickly, he gave the man his whispered instructions, charging him to be vigilant and to speak to no one of his duty save the other men of Darcy's household. Then, he joined Philip, who had already begun checking all the locks on the windows in the common rooms.

When Philip was assured that all was secure on that level, he and Darcy began to check the windows in the family rooms.

"The home is in good repair," commented Darcy as they progressed through the rooms. "I hope it remains so, but I have my doubts it will."

"Tolson will remove anything of value," agreed Philip. "And he will be reluctant to put monies into repairs and improvements."

Darcy paused at a window that looked out over the land attached to Willow Hall. "If only there were a way to save an estate as fine as this from such a fate."

"That, my friend," said Philip, "is beyond what we can do. The property passes to Tolson, and he can do as he sees fit with it. I suspect that if it does not bring him the income from rent that he wishes, he may sell it. It is not entailed."

"Normally, I am not in favour of estates being sold," said Darcy as they entered Lucy's room, "but in this case, I would not only support such an action, but I would also advocate for it." A maid slipped past him with a mumbled apology. From the smudges of soot on her apron and the bucket she carried, he knew that she had been cleaning the grate. "It seems as if the maid has left something behind." He stooped down near the fireplace and picked up a crumpled piece of paper.

"Is it of importance?" asked Philip coming from the window to stand near Darcy.

"I do not know." Darcy began the work of unfolding the twisted paper. "It appears to be a letter." He laid it on the table next to the bed and smoothed the creases as best he could before lifting it to read. He jaw clenched and his eyes narrowed as he read. "She was not just distressed over leaving her home." He handed the letter to Philip.

It took Philip only a moment to read what was written on the paper, but it took him an additional moment along with a second perusal of the missive before he could speak.

"He was here?" Although Philip had read the letter twice, he was, due to the incredulity of the contents, struggling to grasp its meaning. "While we waited below?"

Darcy shrugged. "He may have had someone deliver the letter. Its presence does not equate to his presence."

"Surely, she will not do as he has requested." Philip's eyes scanned the letter again. "How does he have her clothing if he was not here?" he demanded.

"I do not know." He placed a hand on his friend's shoulder. "However, we must not act on presumptions alone. We must first question the staff, and then we must decide how to proceed."

Philip nodded mutely and folded the letter. He looked around the room, her room. It was no wonder she had been distraught. The contents of the letter alone were enough to rattle the nerves, but if he had been here ... Philip shook his head to rid it of the sadness he felt at imagining her fear.

"Come," said Darcy. "She is safe, and we have one more room with windows to secure before we can begin our investigation."

~*~*~

An hour and a half later, Darcy swirled his tea in his cup, watching it rise around the sides and dip in the center. The motion resembled what his mind was doing. He and Philip had questioned every servant; the only one to have seen Tolson was one maid. It was the same maid who had delivered the letter to Lucy, but she had only seen him at the door. She had not seen him enter the house.

It made little sense how a man could enter a house full of people without being seen. But then, the cook had mentioned how her mother had told her about a secret door in the pantry. According to Cook, the door had been boarded up after a particular incident when the younger Mr. Tolson, Lucy's uncle, had been caught hosting a card game in the cellar. He was supposed to have been too ill to accompany his father on business that day and had taken to his room. No one had seen him leave the house, but when his father had gone to look in on him after returning from his business, the room was empty. A search was conducted, and the game was discovered.

And after an examination of the pantry, the door was once again securely nailed closed.

Darcy swirled his tea once more and then drank it. "Do you know what arrangements have been made for the leasing of this place?" Darcy had a very good idea of what the estate would be able to produce if well-tended.

"There is a gentleman named Abbot, who has leased it from Tolson. He has a family — wife, two boys, one is just an infant, I understand. Lucy is to have the house ready to receive him in three weeks time. She said that he seems a respectable sort of fellow, but I have no knowledge of what the financial arrangements are." Philip placed his cup on the table and leaned back in his chair. Darcy's brows were furrowed and his lips pursed slightly. "What are you planning?"

"If I knew what Tolson was to gain from the arrangement, I might be able to make him an offer that would be more advantageous, and his ties to the area would be lessened."

Philip's brows rose. "Purchase Willow Hall?"

Darcy tipped his head to the side as he shrugged one shoulder. "It would be a valuable investment if managed properly, and it would be a good inheritance for a second son." He sighed. "While such an arrangement might satisfy the financial needs of Tolson, I am at a loss as to how to deal with Wickham. I have already given him money in lieu of the living. If I give him more, it will start a never-ending cycle of his coming to me with his hand out."

"Of course, if you do not appease him, he will continue his attacks on your character."

Darcy nodded. "Of that, I am fully aware, but I believe the reprobate nature of his living shall soon deplete his credibility. Attacks on me, I can tolerate to some extent. Attacks on my friends, I cannot." He stood. "Would you care to ride? I would like to take a look at a bit of the land before I plan my offer."

Philip followed Darcy toward the door. "So you are going to do it? Buy Willow Hall?"

"If possible, yes." He turned to Philip. "It would be an excellent wedding gift for Miss Tolson to be free of her uncle, and for you, to see the woman you love more at ease."

Philip's brows drew together. "Lucy would be grateful to be rid of her uncle. It is, after all, the reason we are marrying. It is a matter of convenience, nothing more. She needed an escape, and I needed a capable wife."

Darcy chuckled. "So, you would allow me to marry her instead? I could just as easily keep her from her uncle. She is a gentleman's daughter, and I, like you, am a gentleman's son, so there is no inequality of rank. Her portion is adequate, and she has proven herself very capable of managing an estate. And, I do need a wife."

"Do not be absurd, Darcy," Philip said with some force. An uncomfortable panic began fluttering about in his chest. The thought of losing Lucy to anyone, even a friend as good as Darcy, was surprisingly unsettling. "She and I are already betrothed," he reasoned, "To break a betrothal now would create a stir."

"I could take her to town until the gossip settled." Darcy folded his arms across his chest and leaned against the door, watching the expression of his friend, which confirmed what he already suspected.

Philip pulled in a deep breath through his nose. An unusual desire to hit Darcy caused his hand to clench as tightly as his jaw was.

"Put yourself at ease, Dobney. I have no intention of offering for Miss Tolson. I dare say I would not succeed anyway. She seems rather fond of you." He pushed himself off the door and opened it, motioning for his friend to exit before him.

Philip pondered his response to Darcy's jesting about

offering for Lucy. What had taken hold of his heart? He was not given to violence or even aggression unless absolutely necessary, such as when his sister had been taunted. He may be of a peaceful bent but not when those he loved were in harm's way. He stopped abruptly in the hall causing Darcy to nearly run into him. "I..." he began, shock suffusing his face, "I love her."

Darcy clapped him on the shoulder. "I know. Now, shall we ride?"

Chapter 7

Darcy and Philip drew their horses to a stop as they neared the end of Willow Halls property which was nearest to the village of Kympton and abutted the far reaches of Philip's father's estate. Darcy had been pleased with what he had seen. Purchasing Willow Hall would not be a hardship. The fields were well tended, the pasture land, plentiful for a small flock, and the few fences were in good repair, save for one that Philip knew Lucy had said was to be fixed.

"You say Mr. Callow has been helping Miss Tolson with the management of the estate?" Darcy turned his horse to look back toward Willow Hall.

Philip nodded and following Darcy's lead, also turned his horse. "Since her father trusted him completely, Lucy saw no need for the management to change hands as long as the funds remained to pay him for his service."

"A wise choice." Darcy studied the house before him. It was well-situated with a circular drive. The gardens on either side of the house were not large but were sufficient. The stables, which could just be seen from this vantage point, were large enough to keep several horses. "It is a fine estate."

"Philip! Philip!" Mary Ellen Dobney urged her horse to go faster as she called to her brother.

Philip turned toward his sister, waved, and waited for her to join him. "If you are coming to call on Miss Tolson, you shall be disappointed," he said as she approached. "She is not at home."

Mary Ellen's face scrunched in displeasure for a moment. "I had hoped to find her." She nodded to Darcy. "A pleasure to see you, Mr. Darcy. Were you as disappointed as I am about Lucy's not being home?" She cocked her head to the side, a teasing smile on her lips. "Missing a social call can be quite disconcerting, can it not?"

Darcy rolled his eyes. Were this his friend Bingley's sister, he would be concerned that she was flirting with him, but he knew that Miss Dobney's interests lay elsewhere and she regarded him as a brother. "I was just looking at the estate, Miss Dobney. I fear my disappointment does not match yours as I have already had the pleasure of seeing Miss Tolson today." He chuckled as her eyes narrowed.

"Do either of you know where I might find her? Did she mention where she might be calling?"

Philip glanced at Darcy, who gave him a small nod. "She and her aunt are at Pemberley and shall not return until the morrow."

Mary Ellen's brows rose high in surprise. "She is to stay

at Pemberley?" She drew her horse close to her brother. "There must be a reason," she whispered.

"Not one that you need to know," Philip whispered back.

Mary Ellen gave him a look of displeasure. "I heard some gossip." She stroked the neck of her horse and refrained from looking at her brother. "I know Lucy does not indulge in such things, and neither do I on most occasions."

Philip snorted, earning another glare from his sister.

"But this concerns her...and you." She smiled as both men gave her their attention. "Ah, now you are interested, but I know how you frown on the sharing of gossip, so —."

"Speak." Philip interrupted.

The sternness of his voice startled Mary Ellen. "Her uncle has arrived."

"I know."

"You do?" Surprise suffused her face. "Do you also know that he is here to put a stop to her — your wedding?"

Philip shook his head. "I did not know that, but I do know that where Mr. Tolson goes, trouble follows."

"Trouble, it seems, is named Wickham, for he is following Mr. Tolson." A faint blush crept onto her cheeks. "There is a rumor that her uncle has promised Lucy to Mr. Wickham." She peeked at Darcy. "There is also a rumor that you have used your friendship with Mr. Darcy to secure the living at Kympton, leaving Mr. Wickham destitute and, therefore, hindering the match."

Darcy snorted. "It is Wickham who has left himself destitute, not I."

"Oh, I do not doubt that, Mr. Darcy. I am merely repeating what I have heard." She gave him a reassuring smile.

"Is this all you have heard?" asked Philip. He had noted how his sister continued to avoid looking at him.

She bit her lip and turned worried eyes to him. "No," she whispered, "there is more. Some are questioning Miss Tolson's reputation."

"Why?"

"They say that she has played Mr. Wickham false and that she seems in a rush to marry. They insinuate that she has need of a quick marriage." Her cheeks glowed rosy.

Philip stared at his sister in disbelief. He knew Lucy had mentioned Wickham's implication that just such a thing might happen, but to hear the rumor had already started circulating was rather unnerving.

"I told them it was not so," she said softly, "but you know how gossip goes. The truth is not nearly so interesting a tale as a falsehood." She pulled a small package from her pocket. "I also came to give Lucy this. I found it." She untied the corners of the handkerchief, allowing them to drop open and reveal the necklace inside. "It was her mothers. She will be devastated if she cannot find it."

Philip lifted the necklace with great care. "Where did you find this?"

"Beside her mother's grave." Mary Ellen smoothed and folded the handkerchief. "I suspect she must have left it behind when last she visited, though, for the life of me, I cannot figure out why it was wrapped in her handkerchief. Nor can I figure out why she was not wearing it. The clasp is not broken."

Philip wrapped his hand around the necklace. "I can." He tipped his head toward his sister as he gave Darcy a questioning look.

Darcy nodded his agreement, and so Philip tucked the necklace into his pocket and pulled out the letter. "We found this." He handed the letter to his sister. "It seems Tolson was here."

Mary Ellen raised a questioning brow as she unfolded the letter. Her eyes grew wide as she scanned the letter. "Oh, my. Oh, poor Lucy! " She handed the letter back to her brother. "Oh, I have muddled things, have I not?"

"Not knowingly," murmured Philip as he tucked the letter back into his pocket. His fingers paused for a moment on the necklace before he withdrew his hand. Knowing she had parted with her mother's necklace as her uncle had instructed did nothing to calm Philip's nerves. Instead, it increased his agitation as he realized just how terrified Lucy must have been to receive that letter. It was no wonder she looked ill.

"We have a bit of a plan," said Darcy. "Not much of one really, but enough, I hope. I thought to purchase Willow Hall. It would give her uncle the money he so obviously desires."

Mary Ellen bit her lip and considered the thought for a moment. "But what of the friend mentioned in the letter?"

"Wickham," said Philip.

Mary Ellen's eyes grew wide and her mouth dropped open. "Wickham?" She shook her head. "Of course, his friend is Mr. Wickham. Oh, and I suppose he is also the lover that is mentioned who has an article of Lucy's clothing?" She shook her head again at the scheming. "With the rumors that are already circulating..." She blew out a breath. "It will lend them credibility, and if Mr. Wickham so chooses, Lucy's reputation will be destroyed."

"I assume the article of clothing in question is a chemise." Darcy attempted to not feel the discomfort speaking of such an article of clothing with a lady, but his ears turned slightly red, and he found it difficult not to look away. "Is not one very much like another? It would be difficult to prove that the item belonged to Miss Tolson."

Mary Ellen smoothed the handkerchief on her open palm. "Do you see this?" she asked as she pointed to the design in the corner. "I should not tell you this, as I am sure it is most improper for me to speak of it, but every article of Lucy's intimate apparel bears this design." She ran her finger over it. "It is a beautiful pattern and unique."

She shrugged sadly. "It is why she chose to part with her mother's necklace." She closed her eyes and clutched the handkerchief firmly in her hand. "Oh, I have muddled things!"

"I shall buy it." Philip was studying the ground in front of him. "He wants money. I cannot purchase an estate, but I can buy an item of clothing."

"It will likely cost you far more than any garment should," cautioned Darcy.

Philip turned to look back at the house. "I do not require her dowry. I am not saying that it would not be missed, but its removal will not leave me without means to provide for Lucy or our children."

"It is too much," said Darcy softly.

Philip shook his head and turned to Darcy. "I would give every farthing I owned to protect her. It is not too much."

~*~*~

Lucy pulled the blankets up and tucked them under her chin. It was a cool night and the fire was burning low. She shivered a bit. She wished that she could close her eyes and sleep, but her mind would not allow it. She had yet to think of a solution to her uncle's demands regarding the living. She sighed, turned onto her side, and squeezed her eyes closed in an attempt to sleep.

And there she lay, eyes firmly shut and mind spinning fast for some moments until she heard the door to her room open softly. Though she knew she was safe here, her heart refused to listen and began beating rapidly, and the tears that had been locked away all day started to flow.

"Oh, my dear girl," her aunt said when she placed a hand on Lucy's face and felt the tears that were silently falling. "What is the matter?" She climbed under the covers next to her niece and pulled her close, wrapping her tightly in her arms.

"I miss Papa," whispered Lucy. She wiped at her cheeks with the edge of the blanket. "If he were here, things would not be as they are."

Aunt Tess silently held her and rubbed her back until the sobbing slowed. "Not wanting to leave your home is only natural, and the prospect of marriage can be daunting even to the bravest of ladies."

Lucy shook her head. "It is not that." She wiped her face again with the blanket. "I do not fear marrying Philip. I know he does not love me as I do him, but he will be good to me. I have no doubt of that." She drew a deep shuddering breath. "And I knew I would not live at Willow Hall all my life. Eventually, I would marry."

"Then what is not right?" Aunt Tess continued to rub Lucy's back.

"I should have told you, but I was afraid. He may have heard, and I could not risk it. And then, I thought perhaps I could come to a solution if I just thought enough, but I cannot."

"He?" Her aunt's voice carried much of the same trepidation that Lucy felt as she nodded. "When?"

"Today, just before we left Willow Hall. He came to my room."

"Your uncle was there?" Her aunt pulled back to look at Lucy's face. "He did not touch you, did he?"

Lucy shook her head. "He took mother's book from my bag and a chemise. Oh, Aunt, what will I do? He has threatened to ruin my reputation and my chances of marrying Philip if I do not find a way for the living to be given to Mr. Wickham."

Aunt Tess sat up and propped the pillows behind her. "I am at a bit of a loss, Lucy. Perhaps you should tell me all that transpired during your uncle's visit, and then, we might be able to come to a solution together."

Lucy pulled herself up next her aunt and told her all that happened.

Aunt Tess blew out a breath as Lucy finished her tale. "That is not an easy problem to solve. You know that Mr. Darcy will not give the living to Mr. Wickham even if Philip were to take another position."

Lucy had known it to be true. "But if Philip gives up the position, Uncle will not ruin me."

Aunt Tess shook her head. "He has no scruples, my dear. His word means very little. If he is not satisfied, he will need someone to bear his displeasure, and I do not think him stupid enough to attempt to harm Mr. Darcy. A woman is a much easier victim."

"Then what do we do?" Lucy twisted the blanket in her hand.

Her aunt sat quietly for a moment. "The constable could be informed of the theft."

"Theft?"

"Your mother's book and your chemise."

Lucy's eyes grew wide. "I could not tell Mr. Williams about my chemise, Aunt."

"Your uncle also has your necklace, does he not?"

"But only because I gave it to him. He did not steal it."

"Then the book." Aunt Tess tapped her lip. "It would not be the first time Mr. Williams has been made aware of a delicate matter concerning your uncle. He is a trustworthy man, Lucy. Not a word would leave his lips that would harm your reputation — of that, I am sure." A smile spread slowly across her face. "I believe we might be able to convince your uncle to forget his plans without involving the constable too much." She patted Lucy's leg reassuringly. "It should be enough for your uncle to see Mr. Williams and think that you have reported him. Your uncle escaped before without penalty, but he knows he would not be so fortunate a second time." She climbed out of the bed and waited for Lucy to settle back on her pillow. "You have naught to fear, my dear niece. I shall see that all is put right." She tucked the blankets around Lucy and kissed her on the forehead. "I promised your mother and father that I would care for you, and so I shall until Mr. Dobney relieves me of the position."

Chapter 8

"All will be well," Aunt Tess said as she came to stand near her niece, who was watching the drive to Willow Hall. "Mr. Dobney, Mr. Darcy, and Mr. Williams will all be joining us for tea. We will not be left alone with that man."

Lucy nodded and swallowed. "I am trying to believe you, Aunt, but he is so devious that I fear that even the whole of the king's army would not be enough protection."

Aunt Tess chuckled. "He is not smart enough to out-scheme them all. I have always said that his greed will be the end of him."

"Greed is blinding," Mr. Harker huffed and added, "as is the desire to see the good in everyone. A lesson I've not forgotten since the last time I saw your uncle, Miss Tolson."

Lucy turned from the window and looked at Mr. Harker in surprise.

"Have you not heard the story?" He tilted his head to one side and peered at her as if his eyesight were not dim but fully seeing. "He left the first time under a cloud of rumor."

Lucy came to take a seat near Mr. Harker. "Mother said that he left to avoid being accused of stealing something."

Aunt Tess began the explanation as she took a seat as well. "Two days before he left, there was a theft of some monies from the parsonage."

Mr. Harker nodded. "Your uncle's gloves were found in my study the day the money was taken." He drew a deep breath and released it loudly. "I should have given them to the constable, but I did not. I believed it best to confront your uncle with what I knew, so that is what I did." He shook his head. "He is cunning. His powers of deception are great, for I believed his repentance was real and that like Zacchaeus, he would repay his debt with interest as he promised. I kept his gloves telling him that they would be returned when he had fulfilled his obligation. I still have his gloves, and he has long ago spent my money." He chuckled softly. "I dare say he will not be pleased to see me today." He pulled a glove from his pocket and placed it on the table beside him. "The other is safely stored, but that one should be reminder enough of his past transgressions." He leaned toward Lucy, a solemn expression on his face. "I shall exchange it for the things he has taken from you if you will allow it."

Tears sprang to Lucy's eyes, and though she was certain he did not see the tears, he patted her hand as if he had.

"The Lord has provided for me through the years." He gave a small shrug. "Perhaps He allowed the theft and my deception for such a time such as this." He grasped her hand. "Will you allow it?"

Her head bobbed up and down as she tried to contain her emotions. "If he will accept it," she finally said.

"Good." Mr. Harker leaned back in his chair again but held her hand for a bit longer. "I am a silly old man, I know, but I find I like the idea of having a son and daughter to care for me in my old age." He chuckled. "I know neither of you is actually my child, but I like the idea."

Lucy lifted the hand that held hers and kissed it as she had often kissed her father's hand. "I like the idea as well," she said softly.

"Ah, this is a cozy scene," said Mary Ellen as she entered the room ahead of her brother and Mr. Darcy. "Please, stay seated, Mr. Harker." She placed a kiss first on Aunt Tess's cheek and then gave Lucy a hug and a kiss. "I am afraid I have made things worse for you." She looked at her brother as she took a seat. "I found your necklace and brought it here to return it yesterday."

Lucy's eyes grew wide with fear and her hands knotted in her lap.

"I am sorry, Lucy. I thought you had lost it."

Lucy shook her head. "It is not your fault. How were you to know my uncle had demanded it of me?"

"How were any of us to know?" asked Philip, his voice

77

barely above a whisper. "If Darcy and I had not found the letter, we would still be unaware of your uncle's demands."

Lucy's eyebrows drew together. "You found it?"

"In your room near the fireplace," said Philip, who took a seat next to her on the couch. "We were making sure that all the windows were secure for the evening."

Lucy pulled a folded piece of paper from her pocket and handed it to Mary Ellen, who unfolded it.

"This is from your book of poems, is it not?" Mary Ellen asked.

Lucy nodded. "It was left to me by my mother." She took the page back from her friend. "He has it and has been tearing pages from it every hour as he waits for my reply to his demands." She shook her head and sought her handkerchief. "And he told me that if I told anyone of his visit, he would consign the whole book to the fire." She dabbed in frustration at the few tears which had escaped her eyes. It was not like her to be constantly in tears, but her uncle unnerved her so. "It is why I sent the necklace. I did not want the book destroyed, and I thought it would give me time to figure out what to do." She drew in a breath and forced a smile to her lips. "I have come to no conclusion save that a problem such as this cannot be solved in my own strength."

"Lucy told me of it last night, and Mr. Harker, this morning," said Aunt Tess. "She planned to tell you of it before the constable arrives."

"Mr. Williams?" Darcy asked.

"A bit of strategy," said Aunt Tess. "Lucy's uncle left amid swirling rumors of wrongdoing. Mr. Harker has the evidence needed to prove some of those rumors true. I thought perhaps the presence of the constable may make him uneasy and less likely to cause as large a scene as I expect he might."

Just then, the butler announced the arrival of Mr. Williams, a stately gentleman with full cheeks, somber eyes, and dark hair that was speckled with grey.

"I think it wise to tell him all," said Philip softly as Aunt Tess and Darcy greeted the man and made him comfortable.

"All?" Lucy bit her lip and looked at him in concern.

He nodded.

She slipped her hand under his where it lay on the couch between them. "Then I shall." She waited while Darcy finished his whispered conversation with the gentleman and then proceeded to tell Mr. Williams of everything that her uncle had ever done to her.

Mr. Williams' jaw clenched and relaxed and then clenched again as he considered all that Lucy had told him. He turned his teacup's handle away from himself and then back before lifting it to take a sip. "Well," he said at last, "I believe it is finally time for your uncle to face some consequences for his actions."

Lucy's eyes grew wide in concern.

"No need to fear, my dear," he reassured her as he took another sip of his tea. "I think we can arrange for him to be held accountable without ever mentioning anything of what you have told me today."

There was something very calm and reassuring about Mr. Williams' presence, yet Lucy could not quite rid herself of her fear of both her uncle and public exposure. Her brows drew together as she shook her head. "I do not see how. To convict him of a crime, would I not have to share my story with others?"

Mr. Williams placed his cup on the saucer and returned it to the table next to his chair. "If we went to trial, yes. If your uncle is willing to come to an agreement without a trial, no. We must hope he does not wish to take his chances with a trial. I expect he would be convicted and that the resulting sentence is something he would want to avoid." He sighed. "It does mean, however, that he might still be able to cause trouble in the future if he decides to ignore the agreement."

"We are about to find out," said Darcy from where he stood at the window, watching the front of the house.

Lucy drew a deep breath and blew it out slowly.

Philip gave her hand a squeeze. "You are not alone," he whispered. "I...we will not let any harm come to you."

She smiled at him. "Thank you. How did you know that is what I feared?"

"We have been friends for a long time, Lucy. I know the

twitch of your eye and the flinch of your mouth means you are preparing to stand your ground, and your exhale? That is you trying to shoulder the weight of a situation by yourself." He gave her a half shrug and a smile, which she returned.

Had there not been movement near the door to the room, she would have gladly sat looking into his comforting eyes for some time. The depth of his understanding of her spoke of his care. If he did not love her, at least, she could be assured of his care, and in that, there was great comfort.

"Mr. Tolson and Mr. Wickham," the butler intoned as the two gentlemen, if they could be called that, entered the room.

"I see you have a room full of friends today," said Tolson with a slightly menacing smile on his lips until he saw Mr. Williams and his expression turned hard. "I do hope you have not done anything foolish."

His eye bore into Lucy's. She wanted to look away, but she did not. Today, she would not show him her fear, for although it was there, she knew that she did not have to bear it alone. She had a room full of strength upon which to draw.

"I see you have also brought a friend," she said with as much indifference as she could muster. "Please," she motioned toward some empty chairs as she rose, "have a seat. I will have another cup brought for our unexpected guest." She walked to the door and made the request.

"Tolson," said Williams. "I am surprised you have returned to the area. I do believe I told you just before you left that to do so would be unwise."

"I am sure I have no recollection of such a conversation," said Tolson.

"I recall it quite well," said Mr. Harker. "Did the money you stole from my office get you very far in life? I imagine it was not used on any truly godly activities." He laid the one glove he had brought with him on his knee. Had his eyes been better, he would have seen the colour fade slightly from Tolson's face. As it was, he had to be pleased with the slight rattle of cup against saucer as a sign that he had unsettled the man.

Mr. Williams took the glove from Mr. Harker's knee. "I did not realize it was he who was responsible for that theft."

"Then why did you caution him to not return?" asked Philip.

"That," said Mr. Williams, "has to do with my sister. I believe the caution was that if he returned, I would see him at the end of a pistol."

"She married, did she not?" asked Tolson. Though his tone was one of lack of concern, his eyes watched Mr. Williams uneasily as the man shifted in his seat and leaned toward Tolson.

"She did, but not without some persuasion on my father's part. Some costly persuasion. The effects have been far-reaching, I assure you." Mr. Williams rose and began a circuit of the room. "Mr. Darcy has told me he wishes to make an offer to you. As much as I do not desire to allow any good to come to you, I think it is an acceptable proposal. However, I will assure you that the offer, if refused, shall not be repeated, for I shall have my say after he has completed his." He nodded to Darcy.

"It seems to me that to continually travel to Willow Hall to mend fences and make improvements to the estate will be rather taxing to you, both in energy and finances," began Darcy. "It might be more advantageous to relieve yourself of the responsibility."

"Sell it?" questioned Tolson, a calculating grin forming on his lips.

Darcy nodded. "I know the value of the property, and I am prepared to make a generous offer." He placed a folded piece of paper on the table near Tolson but held it in place with a finger as he continued, "It is not open for discussion or negotiation. It is my one and only offer and must remain between us. Mr. Williams is, of course, aware of the offer, but no one else is. Do you accept my terms?"

Tolson shrugged. "So, I am to say yes or no but nothing else?"

Darcy held his gaze. "Precisely. But first—" He pulled a second paper from his pocket and handed it to Tolson.

"Because your word has been proven to be less than reliable, you must sign this before I show you my offer."

Tolson took the paper and read the same terms on it as Darcy had told him.

"It seems I have no alternative," he grumbled as he accepted a pen and ink from Mr. Williams. Then, having signed his name, he took the folded paper and looked at the offer written on it. His brows rose in surprise. "It is indeed generous." He pulled the corner of his bottom lip between his teeth as he reread it.

"Before you accept," said Mr. Williams, "you should know that I have heard of your visit to Miss Tolson both recently and in the past. I assure you that I will see to it that you do not leave the area should you chose to return again."

"You would kill me?" Tolson laughed.

"Legally and with a length of rope," said Mr. Williams. "I promise you that there are many in this area who would very much like to see any trial end in such a result." He turned to Wickham, who had been watching the proceedings with varying degrees of fascination and trepidation. "I should warn you about your choice of friends, Mr. Wickham, but I fear, a warning is far too late since you are here looking for assistance once again." He returned to his seat. "If you are found to be involved in this scheme to defame Miss Tolson's character, I will stand as second to Mr. Dobney." He leaned toward Wickham. "I assure you there is a reason Mr. Tolson refused to meet me on the field of honour. There is still not a man who can outshoot me."

Wickham nodded rapidly, and Mr. Williams, seemingly satisfied with his response motioned for Darcy to continue.

"Now, then, my offer," said Darcy.

Tolson nodded slowly. "It seems fair."

Williams laughed. "It is far from fair since Darcy is too generous by half," his eyes settled on Wickham, "to both of you."

"You will meet me tomorrow morning at Pemberley before you leave Derbyshire for the final time." Darcy handed Tolson the pen and ink once again.

"It is over," Philip whispered near Lucy's ear. "Everything has been seen to."

"My things?" she asked.

"Yes," he said, "everything."

She drew a deep breath and released it as a smile spread across her face and her heart. She was free. Free of her uncle and his scheming. Free from the fear that had shadowed her since she was that young girl shivering in her night rail. She clasped Philip's hand more tightly. Her lips trembled slightly as happy tears made her eyes glisten.

"You are well?" Philip asked.

She nodded. "I am very well."

"I am glad," he said, giving her hand a final squeeze

before rising to help escort the day's visitors from the premises.

Chapter 9

Mary Ellen handed another book to Lucy. "I am not sure my brother realizes how much of his library at the parsonage he will be forfeiting." She laughed, as Lucy shook her head and rolled her eyes.

"He knows my love of books." She placed the book in the crate and reached for the next. "These are the last of the things I must pack." She and Mary Ellen had been packing for days, but finally, the task was reaching completion.

"I shall be glad to have you for a sister." Mary Ellen could not keep the excitement at the thought from her voice. "We have been nearly sisters our whole lives, but now we shall be sisters indeed."

Lucy laughed.

"Oh, that is a lovely sound," said Aunt Tess. She placed a tray of sandwiches on a table in the library. "I have not heard laughter in far too long."

"I have not been happy in far too long," said Lucy, and then she stopped, the book she was about to place in the crate held in mid-air. She looked at her aunt in concern. "It is not wrong that I am happy, is it? Father has not been gone long."

"Oh, my dear girl," chided Aunt Tess, "if your father heard you, he would give you a sound scolding. Your happiness was always his concern, you know."

"I know, but do I diminish his loss if I do not grieve enough?" She tucked the book in the crate and wiped her hands on her apron before taking a sandwich and curling into a favourite chair — a chair, which after Aunt Tess' whispered information to Philip, was to be taken to the parsonage's library.

"Are you happy because he is gone?" asked Aunt Tess.

"No, I am happy because my uncle is gone," said Lucy. "I miss Papa greatly."

"Then you do not diminish his memory at all. In fact, I would say you do it credit to be able to remember him with sadness but to face life with joy. He would ask nothing more."

Lucy nodded and ate her sandwich in small nibbles as she thought. "Do you think he will return?" she asked a few moments later.

"Your father?" asked Mary Ellen.

Lucy laughed despite the serious look on her friend's face. "No, my uncle."

Aunt Tess shook her head. "He'll not return."

"Indeed, he will not," said Mr. Williams, entering the

library behind the butler. "As Mr. Darcy and Mr. Dobney know, I sent men after Mr. Tolson to make sure he was fulfilling his part of the agreement and leaving the area, which he did. However, it seems your uncle ran into some trouble at an inn. As is his custom, he had indulged in the many vices which can be found at such places, and when returning to his room, he slipped and fell down the stairs. I am afraid he broke his neck and died almost instantly."

Lucy gasped and her hand flew to her heart. "How horrid!"

"An unpleasant way to die to be sure, but not unjust," said Mr. Williams. "My men have made sure that the money he carried, or what was left of it, was taken to his wife and children. From my men's report, there were few tears shed at the news. I believe it was somewhat of a relief to his wife to be rid of him."

Lucy shook her head, her face registering her disbelief. "No one was sad that he had died?"

"Mr. Wickham was rather distraught, at first," said Mr. Williams, "but as soon as my men gave him the things he said your uncle owed him, he was satisfied. I should say I am sorry for your loss, Miss Tolson, but in all honesty, I cannot say that."

Lucy's brows drew together. "I cannot say I am sorry, either," she admitted. "It is very sad — not that he is gone, but that he is gone and there is none who will miss him."

Mr. Williams placed his hat on his head. "I must inform

Mr. Darcy and Mr. Dobney. I wished for you to know first."
He bowed. Lucy thanked him, and he was gone.

Lucy turned toward her aunt after Mr. Williams had left
the room. "He is gone. My uncle is truly gone." She let the
comfort of those words wash over her.

"And your life can start anew," said Aunt Tess.

"As my sister," said Mary Ellen, giving her friend a hug.

"Oh," gasped Lucy, the smile she had been wearing
changing to a look of dismay. "Will Philip still wish to
marry me?"

"Why would he not?" demanded Mary Ellen.

"Because," said Lucy, "he only agreed to marry me to
save me from my uncle, but my uncle is dead. There is no
longer a need to save me."

"Oh, for the love of all that is good," Mary Ellen said,
pulling Lucy to her feet. "Go get your hat."

"My hat?"

"Yes." Mary Ellen stood with her arms crossed and her
toe tapping.

Lucy gave her a puzzled look but did as requested.

"Put it on," her friend said when Lucy returned with her
bonnet. "We are taking a walk."

"But we have books that require packing." There were
only a few shelves left to empty and clean, and she had
expected to have it finished before the afternoon was over.

"Oh, no. Those books will wait. Your foolishness will
not." Mary Ellen grabbed Lucy by the hand and began

pulling her from the room. "I will not let you talk yourself and my brother out of my having you for a sister."

"I do not understand your meaning." Lucy scampered to keep up with her friend's very determined gait.

"You love him, and he loves you." She stopped for a brief moment and gave Lucy a hard stare that prevented her from arguing the point. "But, you do not know he loves you, and he does not know you love him, and since you will assume he is only marrying you to save you, you will think about it for hours and days and finally, you will break off the engagement, thinking you are doing the right thing. And I will be left with not only a very despondent brother and unhappy friend, but I shall be without a sister." Her words fell as quickly from her mouth as her feet fell as she walked. "I will not have my chance of being an aunt taken from me because of your lack of communication."

"Are we to keep up this pace all the way to town?" asked Lucy breathlessly. "Could we not take a horse or the curricle?

"My brother is not in town. He is in the field with Mr. Darcy, inspecting a section of fence."

"Oh," said Lucy softly.

Mary Ellen glanced to the side at her friend. "I will slow my pace if you will promise not to use the extra time to convince yourself that you should not marry my brother." Seeing her friend nod, she slowed down until they rounded a corner and could see the men not far away. Then, she stopped and took her friend by the shoulders. "Do you wish to marry him?"

"I do," replied Lucy.

"And why is that?" Mary Ellen's words were firm but not unkindly so. "I can tell you," she continued without giving Lucy a chance to respond. "It is because you have adored and loved him forever. And that is what you must tell him." She sighed. "He is a man, Lucy. I will allow that he is more perceptive and gentle than most, but he is still a man, and as such, he will not know how you feel unless you tell him. Can you do that?"

Lucy's heart raced at the thought. She shook her head. "I do not think I can. What if he does not love me in return? I could not bear to know that."

Her friend rolled her eyes and shook her head. "If I let go of you, will you stay or will you flee?"

"I will stay?" There was a bit of an uncertainty in her voice as to why her friend would ask such a thing.

"Good, then you will stay here, and I will bring my brother to you." She removed her hands from Lucy's shoulders. "You do not need to tell him that you love him, but if you do, I am certain you will not be disappointed." She pulled Lucy into a quick embrace before waving to her brother and going to fetch him.

Lucy did not flee, but she did take a place in the shade, next to a small wall that ran part of the length of the field before crumbling into ruins, a remnant from years gone by. She plucked a blossom from the flowers that grew around the wall and twirled the flower in her fingers.

"My sister said you wished to speak to me," said Philip as he approached her.

She swallowed and bit her lip as she looked up at him. He had taken out his handkerchief and was drawing it across his face to wipe away the perspiration that was there. His jacket had been discarded, and his cravat hung loosely about his neck. His sleeves were rolled halfway to his elbows, revealing sinewy forearms. She had always found him handsome, and in such a disheveled state, she found him even more attractive. However, instead of spending a few moments admiring him as she wished to do, she turned her eyes toward where his sister still stood with Mr. Darcy and Mr. Williams. "It would be more accurate to say your sister wishes for me to speak to you."

He laughed. "I should have known. What bee has gotten into my sister's bonnet that requires you to speak to me?" Lucy's eyes fell to the flowers she still twirled in her hand. It was not a response Philip had seen from her very often. "You can tell me anything. You know that, do you not?" His voice was soft and reassuring.

She nodded. "It is not that I fear telling you." She peeked up at him. "I fear your response." She drew a breath and released it quickly. "My uncle has died."

"I know."

"So, I do not..." she closed her eyes and her voice grew so soft that Philip had to lean forward to hear her. "I mean, there is no..." Why was it so difficult to say what needed to be said? She chided herself and forced the words out. "You no longer need to marry me to save me from him." Her heart ached as the words fell from her lips.

"You do not wish to marry me?" he asked, taking her hand in his.

Her eyes grew wide, and she shook her head. "I did not say that."

"You think I do not wish to marry you?"

Her nod was small, but it felt in her chest as if that little movement was large enough to cause her heart to crumble like the ruins of the wall next to which she stood.

Philip rubbed the back of the hand he held with his thumb. "You are wrong."

She looked up at him. A tentative smile played on her lips as if she were unsure if she should smile or not. "I am?"

If he was not mistaken, there was a hopefulness to her voice. "You are," he assured her as he took her hand and led her around the end of the wall, so that they were obscured from his sister's view. He knew Darcy would be gentlemanly enough not to spy on him, but his sister was another matter altogether. Over the years, her prying eyes and sharp ears had seen and heard far more than he wished. He was thankful that she had never been given to gossip or tattling.

Once he was safely out of his sister's sight on the far side of the wall, he pulled Lucy into his embrace. As he did so, he sighed. He did not mean to sigh, but it could not be helped. He closed his eyes and savored the feeling of her wrapping her arms about his waist and holding him close.

"I know that we became engaged out of convenience," he began after a moment. "There was a need to protect you, and I was glad to be able to help — very glad." He released his hold on her just enough so that she could tilt her head up to look at him.

"Do you remember the Sunday after the first reading of the banns," he continued, "when we stood in the grave-yard and you asked me how I saw our future?"

She nodded. He had looked so puzzled that day.

"I was thinking how pleasant it would be to have you at my side for the rest of my life, and as you will recall, I told you that I saw our future as happy?"

Again she nodded.

"Lucy, I know it has not been long, but with all that has happened with your uncle..." He drew her close once again, so that her head rested on his heart. "I can no longer think of my future as happy unless you are a part of it. I love you so very dearly, Lucy. And that is why you are completely and utterly wrong about my not wishing to marry you." Once again he could not help the sigh of contentment that escaped him as she squeezed him tightly.

Lucy had wished for a happy life, a life that was both

safe and secure. She had known that with Philip as her husband, she would have all of those things, for he was an excellent man. However, to have him love her was a far greater blessing than she had ever dared hoped for. She pulled back slightly so that she could once again look up at his face. The joy that she felt in her heart shone in her eyes and her smile. "Do you remember the item I left off my list?"

He chuckled. "Indeed, I do." He lowered his head to kiss her, but she pulled back and gave him a teasing smile.

"Before you kiss me..." She tried to look at him while she said it, but her eyes were not so brave as her heart, and she looked away. "You should know that, firstly, I have never been so pleased to be wrong."

He chuckled again, for he knew just how much she disliked being wrong.

"And secondly, you should know that I have loved you since that day when I was ten and you were sent to keep an eye on your sister and me while we gathered berries. You did not want to come, but you did. And you did not make us feel like we were a burden or a chore, although I am certain you must have thought it. You even helped me by tying your handkerchief around my hand when I fell and cut it."

While one arm stayed firmly wrapped around her, he lifted one hand and gently caressed her cheek. "You have loved me for so long?"

She bit her lip and nodded. "Do you still wish to kiss me?" Her heart raced in anticipation of his response and then skipped an entire beat as he caressed her cheek once again, allowing his thumb to pass lightly over her bottom lip.

"Very much," he said. "Very much indeed." And he did.

Chapter 10

One week later, as the birds sang outside in the churchyard and a gentle breeze blew through the open door of the church, Lucy stood next to Philip, her hand joined with his hand as Mr. Harker took his place and began to speak.

"I am reminded of the story of Isaac," said Mr. Harker as he stood before the congregation which had gathered to witness the joining of their vicar and Miss Tolson. "Isaac was in need of a wife, and in order to procure a proper young woman, his father, Abraham, sent a servant back to the land of Abraham's father to find one, for it was not fitting that just any woman should be his son's wife, you see. There were qualifications that needed to be met." He smiled at Lucy, who chuckled to herself and stole a look at Philip.

Philip squeezed her hand and gave her a quick wink.

"The servant was successful in his search," continued Mr. Harker as his attention turned toward Philip. "He found a woman who not only fit the qualifications Abraham had given him, but who also was willing to travel back to his home to marry his master's son." He looked back to the congregation. "As we know, the story does not end there. The scriptures tell us that she became his wife, and he loved her." He paused for a moment and wiped his eyes with his handkerchief.

"The two, who stand before God and me today to join their hands and hearts, are such a couple as Isaac and Rebekah. Mr. Dobney was in need of a wife, one for which I prayed." Again he dabbed his eyes. "Miss Tolson was in need of a rescue."

Several heads nodded their agreement, and a low murmuring of agreement could be heard among the parishioners. Mr. Harker paused to allow for the disturbance, a pleased smile on his face.

After the death of Lucy's uncle, the story of why she had been hastily betrothed to Philip came to light in the form of a lecture given from the pulpit in this very church by the man who stood now performing their marriage ceremony. Mr. Harker had made it clear to one and all in attendance that Lucy's father had instructed her to seek a husband, so that she would not be forced to go with her uncle. The truth about the theft from the parsonage those many years before and the scheming of her uncle in an attempt to gain money for his debauched life had left the church ringing with the loudness of shocked silence. Details regarding her uncle's attack on Lucy's person were, of course, not included. Mr. Harker was quite adept at presenting just enough of the right information to sway the minds of his congregation and quell the rumours that had spread. Apologies in various forms had been made to Lucy and Philip.

As the last whispers died once again into solemn silence, Mr. Harker continued. "It was a marriage conceived in convenience. There was a need and both Miss Tolson and Mr. Dobney were willing to follow the path God had placed before them." He smiled and held up a finger. "Ah, but their story does not end there, for you see, through obstacles and danger, God has drawn these two together," he placed his hand over their joined ones, "first for safety and then for love. God has blessed them both, and I believe He will bless us through them." His face beamed even though his eyes were once again misty and required a drying before opening his prayer book and beginning the formal ceremony.

Before long, vows had been made, prayers had been prayed, the Scripture had been read, and Lucy and Philip stood before their church as man and wife.

"I've something for you," Philip whispered as he led Lucy out of the church. "It is not so much a gift as it is a returning of things which were already yours."

Lucy looked at him, brows drawn closely together in confusion.

"I will explain." Philip shook several hands as parishioners gathered around and followed them to the parsonage where Aunt Tess had arranged a fine wedding breakfast to be spread out on the lawn since the drawing room would be far too small for the number of well-wishers that were expected. He took Lucy's hand and led her around the side of the house and in through the kitchen door.

"Our guests," Lucy protested, pulling slightly on his hand to stop him.

Philip smiled at her attempt and shook his head. "Our guests can wait. This cannot." He led her through the kitchen and into his study. Once she was seated, he took a package from the cupboard behind his desk. "It may not be rings of gold as Isaac gave Rebekah, but I think you will like it just as well." He handed the parcel to her and propped himself on the edge of his desk, his lower lip pulled between his teeth as he waited for her to open the package.

"Oh," she gasped as she folded the paper back to reveal her missing chemise and under it, her mother's book with the torn page tucked back in place. "How did you get them? I thought them both lost when Uncle died." There was a small smile on her face as she ran a finger gently over the cover of the book.

"Wickham gave them to me."

"Gave?" she questioned with raised brows.

Philip shrugged. "He gave them to me, and I gave him some money."

"How much?" She opened the book and looked to see if any pages had been lost from it, but they had not. It appeared to be complete and whole save for the one page that was tucked back in place.

"It matters not, but since I know that look in your eye, I will tell you before you expend as much as one word in attempting to convince me that I am not correct." He chuckled as she swatted his leg. "Six hundred pounds." He smiled to himself as he remembered how he had been able to use the death of Lucy's uncle and the cancelling of what Wickham owed Tolson to reduce the earlier agreed on price of one thousand pounds. Wickham was not pleased with the reduction, of course, but after Philip reminded him that he was coming away from the deal with more money than he would have had remaining of the original amount had Tolson lived, he grudgingly accepted and had parted with Lucy's items.

Lucy's hand flew to her heart and her eyes grew wide. "So much? Surely, that was not necessary."

Philip took the items from her and placed them on the desk before taking her hands and drawing her to her feet and into his embrace. "For you, Mrs. Dobney, there is no price too high."

"But..."

He placed a finger on her lips to stop her protest. "I have already had this argument with Darcy, and I assure you that neither he nor you will convince me that the money was spent in vain, for it has bought back your things and, I hope, something far more valuable, your peace. From this day forward, there is nothing left of what your uncle did which can harm you."

She squeezed him tightly. "How can I ever thank you for such a thoughtful gift?"

He looked down into her eyes, which were peering up at him. "Love me, always, just as you do now."

She shook her head and smiled at him. "I cannot promise not to love you more with every passing day, but I will always, always love you."

"And I, you," he promised before kissing her briefly. "Now, we have guests who are waiting, Mrs. Dobney."

"Indeed, we do, Mr. Dobney," she said as she stretched up and kissed him once more before taking his arm and returning to the garden where she left him to go speak to some ladies and greet his sister.

"Congratulations," Darcy said, coming to stand beside his friend.

"Thank you." Philip grasped Darcy's outstretched hand.

"She liked your gift?"

Philip chuckled. "She did, though she attempted to protest the cost just as you did."

"She was always one of the brighter members of our set," teased Darcy.

"Smart enough to ask me to marry her," Philip replied with a smile.

"I trust I am so fortunate to find such a woman one day."

Though most would not have heard it, Philip did not miss the slightly wistful tone to Darcy's voice.

"You will," he assured his friend, "but she may not be what or whom you expect. I know; I never once considered Lucy as a bride until that day in the cemetery when she asked for my help in saving her from her uncle." He shrugged as he allowed his eyes to follow Lucy where she moved from lady to lady greeting them and making sure they were well-cared-for. "My marriage did not happen as I would have planned, but I am happy for it." He pulled his eyes away from his wife and returned his attention to Darcy. "As Mr. Harker says, God's ways are not always our ways."

"Aye," agreed Darcy, "but they are the best."

"He has said it to you, too, I see."

"Often."

"He is wise." Philip sighed slightly. "I hope that someday I am as wise as he. His role is not easily filled."

"But you will do the office justice, especially with Lucy by your side." Darcy clapped Philip on the shoulder. "I am off to town at month's end to collect Georgiana," he said. "My cousin may also return with me." He sighed. "And Bingley is after me to show him more of estate management. You know, if Bingley did not have an unmarried sister, Willow Hall would be just the thing for him, but as he still has his sister in his care, I am most hopeful that the new tenants will agree to stay at least a year or two. As much as I would love to have Bingley near, I do not desire to be so close to his sister."

Philip laughed. "From what Lucy has told me of the couple, you should have very little issue, if any, with them. I take it that Miss Bingley is still trying to capture you?"

"That she is. No matter how often I hint that her attentions are not wanted or that a connection to trade would not be appreciated by my uncle, she still attempts at every turn to impress me. It really is most vexing."

Philip considered telling Darcy to be less subtle and that a more direct approach might be needed. But he knew Darcy would do all within his power to avoid causing a rift between himself and Bingley until absolutely necessary, so he chose not to say anything about Miss Bingley but rather to comment on her brother's need for an estate. "You must speak to my father. Some school chum of his has an estate in Hertfordshire. He is looking to let it come fall. As I understand it, he wishes to take up a place in town and spend time visiting his daughter and her husband and does not wish to see Netherfield sit vacant."

"Hertfordshire?" Darcy rubbed his chin as he considered the county. "I will mention it to Bingley. I do not see him being ready to take on an estate just yet, but perhaps by the end of this season in town will see him rid of one responsibility." He smirked.

"The season is nearly over, but one can only hope," said

Philip. "And, perhaps, you will be so lucky as to become unavailable to Miss Bingley?"

Darcy shook his head. "You know I have tried to find a wife, but there is none whom I wish to marry." He extended his hand once again to Philip. "I will leave you now. Again, congratulations."

Philip grabbed Darcy's hand and shook it firmly. "Thank you, my friend. We would be honored to have Miss Darcy call when she returns."

Lucy, who had just finished talking with a group of ladies, was at his side and slipping her arm through his. "Indeed, we would. My aunt and I, as well as Mary Ellen, would be happy to supply her with female companionship."

Darcy thanked her and bowed his leave.

"Would you care to take a stroll?" Lucy asked.

"I think we must." Philip lifted the hand that rested on his arm and kissed it before placing it back onto his arm and covering it with his hand. They made a circuit of the lawn, stopping to speak to various individuals and then headed out of the garden and toward the churchyard.

"Papa would be so pleased," said Lucy as they neared the cemetery. "He only wished for me to be happy and secure. It was his greatest fear when he knew his time was short." She stopped and turned to Philip. "Do you wish to join me?"

He shook his head. "Today is your day, but if you would,

please share with him my gratitude for having been on that list of suitors."

"I will." She took a step away and then stopped, looked around and, being certain that they were alone, returned to give him a kiss before scooting away to her father's grave.

Philip leaned against the gate and watched her crouching down and speaking to her father's grave marker. Her hands moved through the air as she spoke, and then she looked back at him, her face radiant with a smile before continuing whatever it was she had to say. He sighed as a deep sense of joy and peace settled in around him. Had it really only been three weeks since he sat on that bench and agreed to marry her? How much his life had changed — and for the better — and all because of... He shook his head and recalled Mr. Harker's words and combined them with his own rambling thoughts. The joy in his soul, the peace in his heart, the woman who claimed his love and returned it in like measure were all due to a marriage conceived, first, in convenience...and then love.

The Tenant's Guest

Willow Hall Romance, Book 2
A Pride and Prejudice Variation Novella

~*~*~

He was checking on tenants. She was visiting family.
Both were about to receive a second chance.

Chapter 1

Derbyshire

The sun cast its warm rays over the meadow and danced its way across the stream as a butterfly took an easy but rambling path from one flower to the next. Leaning against the base of a tree, Elizabeth filled her lungs with air and released it slowly. The summer breeze tugged at her bonnet and willingly, she complied to its suggestion by removing her hat and placing it on the ground next to herself. She closed her eyes and listened to the birds sing for a few moments before turning her attention to her purpose for stealing away from the group of picnickers — the two letters in her pocket.

The first letter was well-worn and treasured even though its contents still caused her heart to ache. It had been many months since she had received it, and yet the words, even now, rebuked her for her foolishness. Such arrogance! Such reprehensible behaviour! Surely, she would be never rid of the shame it made her feel.

Carefully, she unfolded the paper, but she did not read

it. She did not need to. The words were clearly etched in her mind. She only took it out now, as she did so often, to look at the fine writing and think about the gentleman who had written it.

She allowed her eyes to skim over the writing and then rest for a few moments on the signature. She touched his name reverently, tracing each letter, before refolding the letter and tucking it back into her pocket while chiding herself, as she did each time, about her stupidity in refusing such a man.

If she could but go back... if she could choose her words again...but she could not. What had been said, had been said, and words, once spoken, could not be withdrawn.

She drew the right corner of her bottom lip between her teeth, looked across the meadow toward where she knew Pemberley to be, and sighed a small sigh of regret. Part of her wished to see it and perhaps chance upon its owner, while another part of her would like nothing better than to be much further away from any chance meeting with Mr. Darcy. For such a meeting, should it ever occur, was certain to be strained and would no doubt cause her greater pain by reminding her of exactly who it was she had so soundly refused.

It was difficult enough to hear of him, as she had many times since her arrival at Willow Hall. Each time, she felt a further prick of her conscience. He was a good friend, a well-respected landlord, and a fair and just master. She had heard it all — many times.

Slowly, reluctantly, she withdrew her hand from holding the letter in her pocket.

Lucy Dobney had said Mr. Darcy might arrive before the summer's end. Her husband, Philip, had insisted it would be much sooner. Again, a small glimmer of hope battled with an urge to flee at the thought.

She shook her head attempting to clear her thinking. Her mind had been muddled with confusing and conflicting thoughts ever since the evening before she had received this letter — the night when he had declared himself to her.

Regret once again crept into her mind. Perhaps if she had not been startled by his addresses. Perhaps if she had not heard of his part in separating her sister from Mr. Bingley. Perhaps if she had not had a headache. Perhaps then she would have replied in a kinder, more gentle fashion. She forced away the thoughts. What had been said, had been said. What was done, had been done. It would do no good to dwell on what might have been.

She took one last look towards Pemberley and then broke the seal on the second letter. This letter held the promise of much happier thoughts. It was the first Elizabeth had received from Jane since arriving at Willow Hall. Anxiously, she read through the details of life at Longbourn — the calls that had been made, the new baby born to one of the tenants, Kitty's sighing over the absent officers, and the delicacy of the flowers on the material her mother had chosen for a dress. Elizabeth's eyes raced along, searching for the one thing for which she hoped. She smiled and clutched the letter to her chest when she found it. Jane would be arriving with the Gardiners in less than a fortnight! She knew, just knew, that a trip away from Hertfordshire to a land as beautiful as this was exactly what her sister needed to help heal her injured heart.

"Miss Bennet."

Elizabeth opened her eyes to find Mr. Marcus Dobney standing above her.

"Mr. Dobney," she greeted and made to stand.

"Please stay as you were. I shall join you for a moment if you do not mind." He waited for her to give her consent before taking a seat on the grass near her. "I take it you have happy news?"

"Oh, very." She made no effort to contain her excitement. "My sister Jane is to come with my aunt and uncle."

Marcus removed his hat and placed it near Elizabeth's. "So, our company is not enough to keep you entertained?" He affected a severe look that was somewhat ruined by the twinkle in his eye.

She cocked a brow and gave him an impertinent smile. "Indeed, I find the populace to be quite dull."

"Is that so?" He laughed. "And here I thought you were

114

enjoying your stay at Willow Hall. Mrs. Abbot will be disappointed to hear she has failed at being a hostess, and my sister will be greatly displeased to be thought of as anything less than engaging."

Elizabeth could not help the giggle that escaped her as she imagined Mary Ellen Dobney's displeasure. Miss Dobney was not reserved, and often her emotions were evident to all — even when she attempted to contain them. "I cannot keep up such a charade, sir. It is precisely because I find this place to be so lovely that I am delighted to be able to share it with Jane."

"A fine response," he said and then, leaning a bit closer to her, continued in a loud whisper, "I shall not inform my sister or your hostess of their supposed failings."

She gave a quick bow of her head. "I thank you, kind sir." She looked toward the stream where the picnic blanket was spread out on a flat stretch of grass. "You have not come to tell me it is time to depart already, have you?"

"Ah, so you do enjoy the country, do you?"

"I do."

"Then you are in luck. Mr. Harker will not hear of leaving for another half hour at least. He insists that the air will do him and us much more good than sitting about chatting in the house, and I am inclined to agree. My sister insists that some exercise in the form of a walk be taken and has sent me to retrieve you." He took up his hat and rose.

"A lovely idea. I am very fond of walking," said Elizabeth as she folded Jane's letter and tucked it next to the one that was already in her pocket.

She cast a sidelong look at Marcus and considered him for a moment while putting on her bonnet. He was handsome, his manners were pleasing, and his fortune was not without merit. He would be an excellent match — her heart sighed — for someone. As pleasant as he was, she found him of no greater interest than she had found Mr. Bingley. "Oh," she said as, while rising to her feet, a thought overtook her.

"Is there a problem, Miss Bennet?" Marcus looked at her in concern. "You did not wrench an ankle, did you?"

Elizabeth shook her head. "No, I am perfectly well. I was merely thinking about my sister." She placed her hand on the arm he offered. Marcus may not be what she wished for in a husband, but she would not be opposed to having him for a brother.

"I suppose it is far too impertinent of me to ask of what in particular you were thinking?" He smiled down at her as they walked.

"Too impertinent and a trifle ungentlemanly," she answered with a small laugh.

He gave an accepting nod. "Yes, to my father's chagrin, I have always struggled with being more curious and forward than a proper gentleman should be. And my sister will attest to my tendency toward ungentlemanly behaviour." He smiled. "But she is my sister, and, therefore, I am somewhat exempt."

Elizabeth laughed. "Then, Mr. Dobney, we are much alike, but I shall not admit to unladylike behaviour, for foibles in decorum are more readily dismissed for gentlemen than they are for ladies. However, I will concede that my mother has scolded me on more than one occasion for not holding my tongue." Her brows furrowed for a brief moment. "There was some wisdom in what she said, of course. A quick tongue has the potential to cause irreparable damage." Without thought, her free hand slid inside her pocket and rested against Mr. Darcy's well-worn and much read letter.

"So it does." Marcus' agreement was so soft she barely heard it, and when she glanced at him, he was staring ahead with a pensive look on his face.

"Shall I assuage some of your curiosity by telling you about Jane?" She watched as the corners of his mouth turned up once again and his gaze became less focused on the distance, and for a moment, she wished to ask him of what he had been thinking. But having just informed him that such questions were too impertinent, she thought it best to hold her tongue.

"A delightful idea," he replied, "but perhaps we should wait until we have joined the others."

Since they had nearly reached the group, she agreed.

"Have you had good news?" Cecily Abbot, a lady of

about seven and twenty, delighted in having her home filled with people, especially when those people were young ladies she counted as dear friends and relations. She had been anxiously awaiting Elizabeth's reading of the missive. She had speculated about its contents several times since they had left Willow Hall. She was most pleased to have been late in departing, due to an issue with one of her children, for if they had left exactly as they had planned, Elizabeth would not have received the letter until she returned. And such a letter could not be held until later, for it must contain good news.

Elizabeth held out the letter to Cecily. "Yes, it is very good news. Jane shall be travelling with my aunt and uncle." Elizabeth could not help how large her smile grew at declaring such news. It had been lovely of her aunt and uncle to allow her to travel ahead of them when their plans had been altered due to the business at Mr. Gardiner's warehouse increasing and needing his attentions, but she truly did miss Jane.

Mrs. Abbot clapped her hands and accepted the letter, unfolding it to see the good news with her own eyes. "So a week this Thursday?" There was no mistaking the excitement in her voice. "We shall both have our dearest older sisters to keep us company."

She read the letter quickly, exclaiming here and there about some bit of news that the others might enjoy. Then, returning the letter to Elizabeth, she rose from the blanket so that she could join the others on their walk.

"Oh, my. You shall all love Jane as dearly as I do, I am sure," she said to the group. "Am I not correct, Lizzy?"

Elizabeth laughed. "I am rather partial to Jane, so my agreement benefits you little."

"Miss Bennet has promised to tell us all about her sister as we walk," said Marcus. "Perhaps you could assist her, Mrs. Abbot."

"A wonderful idea, Mr. Dobney. I like nothing better than to speak about my favourite people." She turned to Elizabeth. "I am sure that Mrs. Dobney and Mr. Phillip Dobney grew tired of hearing your name as I waited for your arrival." She looked expectantly at her husband, a man six years her senior, who was still lounging on the blanket. "Surely, Mr. Abbot, you are not going to allow me to go away without your company?"

"As shocking as it may be, I think I shall remain here with Mr. Harker." Harold Abbot stretched out his long legs and rested back on his elbows, as he winked at his wife and added, "I will miss you dearly, you know."

"Without a doubt," she replied with a smile.

Elizabeth loved the repartee between Mr. and Mrs. Abbot. They were so very comfortable with each other and those around them. They easily fell into friendship with those they met, and once having fallen into a friendship, they embraced their friends as family — whether they were friends of one day or many years. Such was their attentiveness to their friends that notes would be sent, gifts given, and help extended before so much as a mention of need was spoken. To be honest, it was a skill Elizabeth envied, for although she got on well with most people she met, her disposition was more prone to judge and criticize than to accept.

"You can link arms with me, Mrs. Abbot," said Mary Ellen. "That is if Miss Bennet is content to remain in my brother's care."

There was a bit of a mischievous glint to Mary Ellen's eye and a playful flick of her eyebrow that caused Elizabeth to worry. It was the same as she had seen on more than one occasion when her mother was playing at matchmaking.

"If I had not promised to tell Mr. Dobney of Jane, I should insist upon Mrs. Abbot taking my place." And truly she would have dropped Marcus's arm and insisted Cecily take her place if it had not been for that promise.

"I do not know whether to be flattered or wounded," muttered Marcus.

"Wounded," said his brother, giving Marcus's arm a playful swat.

Elizabeth's face grew rosy. She had not meant for the comment to be anything other than a discouragement to Mary Ellen's scheming.

"Philip," said Lucy softly. "I believe you are making Miss

Bennet feel uneasy, and Mary Ellen." She said no more but gave her friend a stern look.

"Forgive me," said Mary Ellen. "I should not have teased."

"Indeed," said her eldest brother. "Mary Ellen is as much a trial to my father as I am at times when it comes to minding our tongues, but we cannot all be as good as Philip."

"I find I am in agreement with you, Marcus," said Lucy, smiling and leaning into her husband's side just a bit more.

The comment sent a chuckle around the group as they set off on what would be a very lovely half hour.

Chapter 2

The Dobney's barouche was the first to arrive at Willow Hall. As they turned into the small circular drive, Elizabeth noted, before her view was obscured, that a fine carriage stood in front of the house. She must not have been the only one to have noticed the carriage, for she heard the hastening of horses from behind them.

"I see the Abbots have a new guest," Mr. Dobney said with a smile.

"Oh, so they have." Mary Ellen waved to whoever was behind their carriage as the horses came to a stop. "Philip and Lucy will be pleased."

Elizabeth wished to turn around and look to see who this newcomer was but did not wish to appear unladylike and so she sat, waiting until Mr. Dobney would hand her out of the carriage after his sister.

"I had not expected to see you for another month complete." Elizabeth could hear Mary Ellen greeting the visitor as she placed her hand in Marcus's and began descending the steps.

"I had not expected to return, but Georgiana was home-sick for Pemberley, and so I indulged her."

Elizabeth's step faltered, and she stumbled slightly while her mind flew toward the voice and away from its job of helping her feet reach the ground gracefully. Her heart beat wildly inside her chest. He was here, standing just out of sight behind the raised canopy of the carriage.

"Are you well, Miss Bennet?" Marcus asked in concern.

"I am, thank you. It was just a small misstep." She flashed him what she hoped was a reassuring smile. Her body felt strangely numb while her mind seemed to be running in circles. She did not even notice how Marcus, who was still looking at her in concern, tucked her hand into the crook of his arm to ensure her safety. She was far too busy contemplating the man on the other side of the carriage and attempting to listen to the conversation.

"Oh, that is the best news," Mary Ellen was saying. "She will have to call on us all as soon as she is settled — and you may accompany her if you wish."

There was a small masculine chuckle of amusement in response to the comment, and Elizabeth nearly stumbled a second time. It was a pleasant sound and one she had not heard before. The Mr. Darcy she knew had not once appeared amused. He had been so serious and very ill at ease. But here, she noted as she stepped out from behind the carriage, he appeared to be quite the opposite. Here, he was smiling and relaxed.